Ras<

Raccoon Riot

Ruff McPaw Mysteries

Book 9

Max Parrott

Contents

Chapter 1

Angela Atkinson leaned against the horn on the steering wheel of her black SUV.

Beep!

The leaves on the nearby oak rustled overhead, and she cringed as a flock of turtle doves took off into the crisp winter air, shattering the serenity of the otherwise peaceful neighborhood.

Ruff McPaw, her trusty border collie, best friend, and dog in crime, whined from his spot in the passenger seat and buried his face in his paws. He tilted his head and glared at her.

Seriously? Do you have to force this old bucket of bolts to make that horrendous sound?

He barked softly, and a low growl emitted from his throat. He had keen senses in the first place, being a dog and all, but since he officially became Angela's right-hand dog and a private investigator, he liked to think they'd gotten even stronger. His expert nose and extra-sensitive ears had been essential in cracking more than a few of Angela's toughest cases, but there were times, like now, when they could be seriously annoying.

Another minute went by, and Angela let out a long breath as she honked again, craning her neck toward the front door of her best friend Michelle Blackfoot's house. The curtains covering the windows didn't ruffle, and neither Ruff nor Angela could see any movement from inside the house.

That's odd. Ruff barked softly as he scanned the yard. Michelle was the editor-in-chief of the Hummings Hollow Gazette and was rarely late. Punctuality was always important, but Ruff thought it would be even more so today, of all days.

Angela leaned on the horn again, wincing as Ruff whimpered louder this time, trying to whack her hand away. She knew he hated the sound, but if they didn't hurry, they were going to miss the beginning of the auction.

"I know, boy, I'm sorry," Angela reached over to scratch behind Ruff's ears. "I know it's loud for those doggy ears of yours."

Ruff huffed, his hot breath fogging the passenger side window. *You have no idea. It's like torture. Now my head is ringing!*

A few seconds later, though, her persistence paid off and the front door of the house swung open. Michelle rushed out, weighed down by an overstuffed purse and a towering pile of books and papers that looked ready to topple from her arms at any moment. Angela swung open the passenger door to let Ruff hop into the back seat.

"What on earth are you wearing?" Angela stifled a laugh as Michelle crammed herself into the front, trailing scarves, and the musty smell of mothballs along with her. Her long black hair was pulled back into a neat bun, and a large pink hat that looked like it had come straight out of Victorian England obscured her dark brown complexion.

Michelle rolled her eyes. "I've been a journalist long enough to know that if I'm gonna go undercover, I have to look the part."

Angela shook her head but allowed Michelle to buckle up as Ruff hopped into the backseat. He growled at the makeshift service dog vest draped across the seat and Angela clicked her tongue. "If you want to get into that auction, mister, you're going to have to suffer through wearing that vest for a few hours." He hated the vest and Angela wasn't proud of it, but it was the only way to get him into otherwise restricted areas. Besides, if she left him at the farm without a good reason, he would sulk for who knew how long.

He huffed, but settled down to lie horizontally across the back seat. *The things I do for a case.*

"Sorry, I'm so late," Michelle said as she shifted in her seat. "I just got so caught up researching the forgery ring. Did you know Sterling has a business partner who—"

"Tell me on the way," Angela interrupted as she stifled a grin. She shifted the car into drive and peeled down the street. "We've got to move if we're gonna make it to the auction on time."

Rumors had been swirling for years that many of the high-ticket items at Sterling's exclusive antique auctions were forgeries, but the man changed aliases every time the police came around. By the time they tracked one down, the man's history had been all but wiped out. He had done it so many times that more than a few police departments were beginning to doubt if the man and his ring of swindlers existed at all. But a few weeks ago, just after Thanksgiving, Michelle had gotten an anonymous tip about an exclusive antique show making a stop in Hummings Hollow.

Of course, she immediately told Angela, and when Chief Helbar caught on, it was all hands on deck for a sting operation. As they turned the corner, Angela glanced down at the Manila file her father had given her before she left that morning. This had been a cold case since he was on the force with Chief Helbar, and he was determined to see it solved, maybe more than Angela herself.

But if this was the case even Charlie Atkinson couldn't solve, Angela hoped the chief was better prepared. Her father was one of the best cops she knew and though he had been the first one of the two of them to turn in, his dedication to solving crime never quite went away. Her fingers itched to go over the details of the file one more time, but as the light ahead turned green, they had no choice but to move forward.

As they pulled up to the hotel entrance, Angela glanced over and spotted the eager sparkle in her best friend's eyes. She'd been plenty of help on previous cases, but this was her first official sting operation. If her outfit and incredibly overzealous planning weren't a dead giveaway of her excitement, Angela didn't know what was.

Thankfully, Michelle left most of her painstaking research in the car, only taking what she could fit into her purse (which was, surprisingly, a lot).

"Come on, you know the drill." Angela stepped onto the pavement and clipped the vest in place as Ruff grumbled.

Officer Kimberly Dell, a young African American beat cop who was rumored to be the top officer in the running for Chief if Helbar retired, marched up to them as they approached the entrance of the building, Angela kept tight hold of Ruff's leash as he strained at the overwhelming barrage of scents assaulting his nostrils. Streams of people of all ages, including businessmen, bargain hunters, and everything in between, pushed past them in droves, fighting to be the first one through the doors. Ruff's senses were in overdrive as he fought to discern all the distinct smells and sights, but he grinned at the sight of his favorite officer. Kim was fully decked out in hotel security garb, so she was almost indiscernible from any other employee.

Ruff pounced on all fours, resting his paws on Kim's shoulders and covering her face in sloppy kisses as Angela tugged on the leash. "Whoa! Down boy,"

Officer Dell laughed as she patted him, before discreetly pressing onto both of his shoulders until he relaxed and landed on all fours.

"He's certainly excited," Officer Dell chuckled.

Michelle clutched her purse a little tighter and tried to hide her smile. "He's not the only one," she hissed.

Kimberly grinned and led them inside, waving them over to a quieter corner under the guise of checking their bags before saying anything else. She slipped Michelle's giant purse off her arm and pretended to check their bags while sliding two earpieces into each of their palms. "These are wired to the chief and Townsend in the surveillance van," she whispered as she glanced between them. "Hook them up and do a quick mic check before you head inside. That way, they'll be able to hear you if anything goes wrong. Do you both remember the plan?"

Angela and Michelle exchanged significant glances and then nodded. Angela would keep tabs on Sterling, while Michelle mingled with the other auction patrons and try to chat them up to uncover any accomplices. Both would keep an eye out for fake antiquities up for auction.

Officer Dell pressed her lips together and squeezed Angela's shoulder. "Remember, I'll be right out here."

Angela smiled, but nodded resolutely. "Don't worry, we got this."

After one last check that all the technology was up and running, Kim led them back into the fray, allowing them to be whisked away with the crowd.

Just then, Chief Helbar's voice crackled through her earpiece. "Atkinson? Blackhoof? What's your twenty? The auction is set to start any minute. Do you have eyes on Sterling Hastings yet?"

Angela pressed a hand over her earpiece. "Not yet. We're on our way, Chief."

The chief huffed on the other end of the line. "Well, what are you waiting for? We don't have all day."

Angela nodded, then clasped Ruff's leash a little tighter and beckoned Michelle forward as they melted back into the crowd. They trailed a few feet behind a man in a fifties-style suit and took the elevator up to the ballroom floor. Eerie chamber music echoed from behind the solid oak double doors.

Holy dog biscuits. So many smells. Ruff quivered against Angela's leg as he lifted his nose into the air. Wood polish, mothballs, champagne, fur, and... too many other things to name. His nails caught on the carpet as they inched closer to the door.

"Chief, I think we found it." She reached for the door handle and Michelle's palm turned clammy in hers as she twisted the metal and pushed it open.

"Relax," she said softly. "Just... channel your inner actress and try to have fun."

Michelle swallowed and let out a hoarse laugh. "Right... fun," she muttered, and Angela couldn't help the small smirk that slid onto her lips. It took a lot to get her friend flustered, but she supposed she couldn't blame her for being nervous.

Once her eyes adjusted to the dim lighting, Angela swallowed back a gasp. The room had been fully transformed into a showroom like something straight out of a home decor magazine. Displays housed antique furnishings, artwork, jewelry, watches, and countless other trinkets, all illuminated by the glow of mini-spotlights. Waiters in white gloves circulated the room, carrying trays of champagne and hors d'oeuvres and the crowd was so thick Angela could barely make out anything but the other patron's silhouettes.

At the center of it all, visible only because he had taken up resistance on the wooded platform a foot off the ground, stood Sterling Hastings. He wore a sharp tuxedo, and his salt-and-pepper hair was perfectly combed. Sterling was older than Angela expected, but still handsome. He greeted every guest with a firm handshake and a wide smile, but Angela didn't miss the snake-like glint in his pale gray eyes.

"Hello, beautiful people!" The crowd broke out in a muted wave of applause and his grin grew impossibly wide as he gestured to one of the passing waiters with a flourish. "It's such an honor to have you all here today. Feel free to enjoy the hors d'oeuvres while perusing our catalog. The live auction for our premier pieces will begin shortly."

Everyone dispersed, and Angela squeezed Michelle's hand. "OK," she whispered. "This is it. Put on your expert reporter hat and do your thing."

Michelle pressed her lips together in a thin smile, let out a shuddering breath, and rolled her shoulders back. "Right. I got this."

"Of course you do," Angela said, nudging her shoulder. "Just think of it like another day at the office."

As her friend set off with her reporter's notepad in hand, Angela made her way through the maze of displays. One intricate blue and white vase depicting pastoral scenes caught her eye. As she leaned down to inspect it, a gruff voice rang out.

"You'd have better luck finding authenticity in a flea market trash heap," scoffed Victor Callahan, owner of the Hummings Hollow Antiques.

Angela raised an eyebrow. "Well, aren't you full of holiday cheer?"

"I call 'em like I see 'em. And I'll tell you one thing: most of what Hastings has trotted out this year is about as real as a politician's campaign promises. The only thing I'm even remotely interested in is that epergne over there." He pointed, and Angela swiveled around to follow his gaze to a beautiful centerpiece on the table near the auctioneer's podium. It was a beautiful glass sculpture interwoven with patterns in every shade of the rainbow, and when it caught the light just right, mesmerizing patterns danced along the wall.

"Wow," Angela murmured.

Victor nodded. "A regular of mine has been searching for this piece for years. Even went diving into the black market for it." He shifted on the balls of his feet and glanced around nervously. "Believe me, Miss Atkinson. I don't like this any more than you do. But it's a family heirloom, and you know how much I care about keeping my reputation with my customers."

Angela's jaw dropped slightly. She always knew Victor Callahan was a very dedicated man, but to see him go to such lengths for his business... was more than a little surprising.

"Is it real?" She raised an eyebrow and tried to push closer to inspect it, but was blocked by an influx of shoppers crowding around the auction table. Victor followed close behind, a small smirk curling up his lips as he scoffed.

"That, Ms. Atkinson, truly is the million-dollar question."

"Now Victor, no need to disparage these treasures prematurely! I only acquire items of the highest caliber for my curated events."

Angela stiffened under the sudden pressure of a hand on her shoulder, and she whirled around, only to come face to face with Sterling Hastings himself. A low growl emitted from Ruff's chest, but Angela rested a comforting hand on the top of his head and shot him a pointed look.

Easy, boy, she thought. *We don't want to make him suspicious.*

"Whatever you need to tell yourself, Sterling," Victor muttered as he glanced at his watch. He sighed, then looked around again, scrutinizing every inch of every trinket within seeing distance with the same critical eyes, sliding past the stalls as if it was no different from perusing the town flea market.

Odd, especially considering his apparent disdain for the man in front of them.

"Is this auction going to start soon, or are you just trying to keep us here until your motley crew of lemurs bleeds themselves dry on your junk?"

Sterling's smile became tighter, and something dark glinted in his gaze. "I assure you, Callahan, the auction is due to start any minute. Feel free to peruse any of our tables while you wait."

Chapter 2

Victor gave Sterling a long look before he finally stalked off, and Angela did her best not to stiffen when the latter's icy gaze met hers. He mopped some sweat from his brow with a kerchief from his pocket and coughed into an elbow before his expert salesman veneer slid back into place. Sterling looped an arm around her shoulders and led her down yet another row of treasures. "Never mind what a curmudgeon like Victor Callahan thinks. I can tell you're a woman with excellent taste. Seeing anything that catches your interest?"

Angela flashed a polite smile. "I'm shopping for my mother today. She adores European antiques," she lied. "I don't suppose that decanter set over there is reasonably priced?"

Sterling's eyes went wide as they darted over to the sparkling, crystal-cut Waterford Lismore. It had a long, slender neck and rounded body complete with a crystal stopper, and despite everything the chief had warned her about, it truly seemed like an exquisite piece. "You have a keen eye for detail," he said smoothly, clearing his throat as he shuffled over to the table and plugged the decanter right off the display as he sighed with mock regret. "Unfortunately, this is not for sale. It's precious to my lineage, and I can't bear to give it away, even for the right price. But perhaps if you impress me with sufficiently spirited bidding later, I might part with another of my treasures that are only reserved for my most esteemed, exclusive customers."

Angela laughed lightly. "I'll keep that in mind, sir. Thank you for the preview."

He nodded and sauntered away. Angela followed a few paces behind him as he tried to disappear into the crowd and the chief barked over her earpiece.

"You got him yet?"

Angela darted to a dark corner of the room and mimed brushing some of her long blonde hair behind her ear as she cupped her hand around it. "Yes. No solid evidence he's anything more than a pawn so far, but I'll keep you posted."

The chief grunted into her ear. "I'm going to hold you to that," he muttered.

Angela nodded.

Over the next hour, Angela took meticulous notes as she watched Sterling interact with his "esteemed guests". For the most part, he seemed to be every bit the charming and suave salesperson he had presented himself as when they first met. Though, every once in a while, his gaze would dart around the room as if he were scanning for security personnel or suspicious individuals.

Michelle found Angela again by a display of 19th-century Dutch paintings. "Quite the buzz around that screen set," she whispered, gesturing vaguely across the room to a wood-painted screen woven with intricate flower designs. "Do you think it's a fake, too?"

Angela nodded. "I've also heard he has some 'Fabergé egg' replicas that appear to have miraculously found their way from a collector in France."

"Miraculously indeed," Michelle snorted. "Here's to hoping I can help you guys finally pin this eel and the rest of his operation down for good."

Angela's gaze wandered to the makeshift stage in the center of the room, where Sterling had stepped up behind the podium.

"Heads up," she whispered. "I think it's showtime."

As the attendees funneled into the rows of folding chairs facing the low stage and auctioneer's podium, Angela and Michelle seated themselves front and center. Sterling welcomed everyone with a bit too much enthusiasm, and his flush cheeks left Angela wondering if his performance was from excitement or desperation. After introducing his associates manning the phone banks and making a few cheerful introductory remarks, the bidding began.

"Stir the pot," Officer Townsend hissed into her earpiece. "Keep an eye on the highest bidders. When this is all over, maybe we can see if any of them know more than they are letting on."

Angela and Michelle met each other's gazes and nodded resolutely. "On it," she whispered.

They leaned forward and began bidding with gusto, and though none of them won (thank goodness), she noticed several patrons giving her the stink eye from across the room: a man wearing a fedora, a woman in a coat that looked suspiciously like real tiger fur, and a girl who couldn't have been much older than Kathy wearing a necklace that looked way too expensive for someone her age.

Sterling was also staring; though she couldn't be sure whether it was out of pure curiosity or if he was becoming suspicious.

When a jade Buddha statue came up for bid, Michelle jumped in, raising Angela's initial bid by a full thousand dollars. As a few other bidders joined in, a new sheen of sweat broke out on Sterling's forehead, and he stumbled a bit as he continued calling out numbers. Each time the bid went up, no matter how many increments, Sterling's smile grew impossibly wide until it turned into a strained grimace.

Angela leaned forward when his hand twitched with spasms, and his gaze darted around the room. He continued calling out numbers, but with each bid, his pace grew more and more stilted as larger spasms contorted his limbs.

"Something's off." Angela hissed into her earpiece. "He either knows we're here and is searching for a way out, or..." she trailed off.

On stage, Sterling's grip on the podium whitened his knuckles. He tried to disguise a violent shudder behind an exuberant mask, but Angela didn't miss the way his voice cracked when he said, "The energy here is overwhelming!"

"Or what, Angela?" Officer Townsend prodded.

Angela's brows furrowed. "I'm not sure. He looks like he's coming down from a high or something."

The chief's voice crackled in her ear. "Being a possible drug addict doesn't give us reason to move in," he huffed. "Call when you have actual evidence."

The line went dead, and Angela sat back. Every bone in her body was telling her they were missing something. She just hoped they would recognize it before it was too late.

Chapter 3

Soon enough, the epergne came up for auction. Before Sterling could even finish introducing it, Victor vaulted to his feet, engaging in a fierce bidding war with another customer. Sterling fought to keep up, but it was like watching a tennis match stuck on warm speed. The second he announced each bid, the other person would outdo it by at least five hundred dollars.

"Well, well, it seems we have some serious collectors among us this afternoon!" Sterling huffed, tugging at his collar.

Angela's phone buzzed. She glanced download and was relieved to see a new text from Kim.

The team is on standby. Keep us updated.

On it.

Angela sent the message off with a satisfying whoosh, but her gaze flew toward the stage when Michelle's nails dug into her arm.

"Angela," she hissed. "Look!"

They watched in horror as another spasm shook Sterling's body. This time, he nearly collapsed. He steadied himself on the podium and, forcing out one more, much too painful to be a genuine smile, declared, "sold to Mr. Callahan for fifteen thousand dollars!"

Angela frowned as Sterling loosened his tie, blinking rapidly as he wiped his brow and stumbled against the podium.

"Pardon me, ladies and gentlemen, I'm... feeling rather unwell all of a sudden." He motioned to the side of the stage, and a man in a charcoal gray suit with an auburn toupee stepped up to the podium. "I need to step back for a moment, but my colleague Conrad will take great care of you until I return."

Angela and Michelle exchanged glances as Sterling hurried off stage. Murmurs rippled through the crowd and Conrad tried his hardest to maintain order, but it was to little avail. The crowd shifted restlessly, and Conrad's eyes darted back and forth between the front rows and the back doors Sterling had stumbled out of moments before.

Angela nudged Michelle on the shoulder. "I'm going to go check out his dressing room and make sure he's not about to pull a disappearing act on us."

Michelle nodded and agreed to let the chief know what was going on

Angela sprang from her seat and walked as quickly as she could toward the same back door from which Sterling had exited. She made it out into the hall just enough to glimpse the back of Sterling's head as he darted down the side hallway toward the men's lockers, which were right near the back door exit.

"Chief," she hissed into her earpiece. "He's heading toward the men's locker room. Block him off by the right back exit."

"Got it,"

Angela stayed a few paces behind to avoid appearing too suspicious. Her pulse slowed slightly when, instead of heading for the bright red exit sign blinking straight ahead of them, Sterling turned a sharp corner and pushed into the men's locker room. She paused just a few feet outside the door and waited for her labored breathing to even out before radioing the chief.

"Never mind. He's still in the hotel. He went into the men's locker room."

"Well, what are you waiting for?" The chief barked. "Go see what he's doing! If he caught you tailing him, he might try to make a break for it through a window."

Angela scrunched her brow. She highly doubted that was a possibility, considering they were at least a few floors up. Sterling may have looked good for his age, but he never struck her as the exceedingly athletic type. Still, Angela didn't want to waste time arguing, so she simply nodded. "All right, I'll let you know what I find."

Angela braced herself before pushing open the men's locker room door. "Sterling?" Her voice left a tinny echo along the slick locker room walls, ricocheting off the metal. Ruff sniffed the air and then pressed himself onto her side. Nothing smelled out of order, but something definitely wasn't right. Goosebumps rose on Angela's arms when she was met with only silence. Ruff whined as Angela gently tugged on his leash and they ventured further into the dimly lit room. They rounded a corner and Angela's breath caught in her throat, blood running cold. Her gaze landed on Sterling, slumped over on a chaise lounge in the center of the room. His back rested against the wall, his once labored breathing now eerily still.

"Sterling?" Angela whispered as cotton coated her mouth. She approached him with slow, cautious steps, high heels clicking ominously against the tile floor. Reaching out, she gently shook his shoulder. "Mr. Hastings?"

Still nothing.

She took a deep breath, then reached out with two trembling fingers to feel for a pulse, first at his wrist, followed by his neck. Nothing. Her stomach twisted into a tight knot as she cupped one hand around her earpiece.

"Chief."

"Where is he, Atkinson? I thought you said he was headed toward the left side of the building." Chief Helbar's gruff voice crackled through the speaker, and she winced.

"He was." Angela gulped as her gaze drifted back toward his lifeless body. "I'm not sure what happened, but it looks like... he may have committed suicide."

Chapter 4

"What in the world..." Chief Helbar let out a long breath as he surveyed the scene. Kim stepped up beside him, pulled latex gloves from her pocket, and made notes on a small pad. "Window is locked from the inside. No disturbances that I can see."

The chief's eyes blazed and his mustache twitched above his tight frown as he whirled on Angela. "What happened?"

Angela shook her head and pushed to her feet as he ambled up beside her. "I don't know. Sterling looked a little clammy earlier, but I thought it was just nerves. I'm wondering if someone tipped him off that we were here, especially with the way he rushed off the stage. Maybe he didn't want to get caught and thought this was his only way out?"

Ruff whined softly. It made sense, but somehow, he doubted it was that simple. None of their cases ever were.

The chief grumbled something unintelligible as he approached Sterling's lifeless body and put his own fingers on the man's neck as he checked his watch. A second went by, followed by another.

The chief cursed under his breath and raked a hand through his hair. He cleared his throat and turned toward Kim.

"Get the coroner down here," he said gruffly. "And someone search the room for a suicide note." Both Kim and Officer Townsend nodded. Kim pulled out her phone and immediately dialed Dr. Caldwell, while Officer Townsend moved in to inspect the crime scene. Meanwhile, Chief Helbar pulled Angela aside.

"Are you sure you remember nothing else about the way he behaved at the auction? Did he seem drunk when you talked to him? High maybe? Intoxicated in any way?"

Angela pressed her lips together and shook her head. "Not really," she mused. "Like I said, he seemed warm. His cheeks were red, and he was constantly mopping his forehead..."

The chief nodded. "Both classic signs of someone who has been using, but probably hasn't had a hit in quite a while."

Angela hummed. "But how long would it take for someone to go through withdrawal?"

The chief clicked his tongue. "Depends on how hard they've been leaning on their crutch. Sometimes a few hours, sometimes a few days. I'm assuming Sterling wanted to be sober for the auction. But until we get the medical examiner's report back, we won't know anything for sure."

They turned back to the crime scene, and Angela raised her eyebrow when Officer Townsend came closer to them.

"Any luck?"

He shrugged and held up empty hands. "Not so far." The tile squeaked like nails on a chalkboard as he swiveled on his heel and glanced at Kim.

"Anything?" he called out.

Kim stood from where she had ducked beneath the chaise lounge and shook her head. "Nothing here."

Let me try. Ruff sniffed the air and strained at the end of his leash. The cloying scent of alcohol lingered in the air, and he wanted to know where it came from. He padded over to the chaise lounge and jumped up next to Sterling's body.

"Ruff, no!" Angela and Chief Helbar raced over, but the shift in weight had already jostled Sterling's body. He slumped over on his side, and something fluttered out of the front pocket of his suit jacket.

"Stay back, Ruff!" Chief Helbar barked. "This is a crime scene."

Ruff whined but obeyed and jumped down, still eyeing the scene.

Angela leaned forward but stopped short when the bitter tinge of alcohol wafted up her nose as she bent down near the body to pinch the small item–an old, torn photo, between her fingers. She turned it over. It was grainy, and much of the image was barely discernible. But she could make out the distinct glitter of the Waterford Lismore whiskey decanter, the same one she'd seen earlier that Sterling claimed wasn't for sale. There was something scribbled on the back of the photo, but she couldn't quite make it out.

"Officer Townsend?"

He turned. "Find something?"

Angela frowned as she squinted at the scrawled handwriting. She was more than a little positive it didn't belong to Sterling. It was far too elegant. Not to mention far too short to have acted as a suicide note. "I'm not sure yet... but maybe."

She held out the photo, and Officer Townsend retrieved an evidence bag from the kit he always carried, carefully slipping it inside. "Nice catch. We'll inspect it at the office."

Angela nodded, then cringed when she turned to find the chief tugging far too timidly on Ruff's leash to get him away from the crime scene. "Kimberly," he grunted. "Take him back to the van. These quarters are too cramped for him to poke around without contaminating the crime scene."

Excuse me?

Ruff huffed indignantly and glanced at Angela, who sighed but reluctantly nodded. "Sorry, boy. The chief has a point. The coroner's gonna be here soon though, so maybe you can come back after he's done?"

Ruff growled softly, but thankfully didn't put up too much of the fight when Kim stepped in to take his leash. "Come on, boy. It'll only be for a little while."

They trotted out of the room. Angela watched them go but barely had time to turn back for a second look at the crime scene before–

"Sterling? Are you still here? People are asking questions about–" Angela's eyes snapped up as the man with the toupee stepped inside, brow furrowed. The rest of the words died in his throat as he caught sight of Sterling's lifeless body sprawled on the chaise lounge, Chief Helbar, and Officer Townsend hovering nearby. "What the devil happened?"

"Conrad, right?" Angela stepped forward and held out her hand. "I'm Angela Atkinson." The man stiffened, his chest rose and fell unsteadily as he fought to absorb the scene before him. A million emotions–confusion, horror, anger, and something else Angela couldn't quite read flashed across his face.

He gripped her hand a little too tightly as he finally found his words. "Um, yes. Hi. I'm... I'm sorry, but... what are you all doing here?"

Angela's gaze softened as she gestured toward Chief Helbar. "We're so sorry to bombard you like this, but it seems Mr. Hastings suffered some kind of overdose."

"Overdose?" Conrad echoed, eyes wide as they darted between Angela and the officers behind her. "What are you talking about?"

Angela sighed. "I noticed he wasn't feeling well during the auction. When he left the stage, I went to check on him. He turned in here and when he didn't come out after a few minutes, well..." her eyes drifted black to Sterling, still slumped on the lounge, eyes wide and unseeing, "I found him like this. I'm not sure what happened, but I smelled alcohol on his breath, and there's no pulse."

Shock settled into Conrad's features. He opened and closed his mouth several times, but nothing came out.

Chief Helbar stepped forward, pulling out his notebook and flipping to a fresh page as he rubbed his mustache. "Believe me, Mr. Cummings," he said, his tone surprisingly devoid of his usually gruff edge. "I know this is a lot to take in, but the more we know now, the less we have to revisit this in the future." That seemed to be enough to snap Conrad out of his stupor. He shook his head and blinked as if seeing the chief for the first time.

"Oh, of, of course."

The chief nodded and began scribbling in his notebook. "Good. Now, did your friend have any addictions that we should know about?"

"Addictions?" Conrad repeated, frowning. "No, none that I can speak of. He didn't even drink regularly. He gets a bit of stage-fright sometimes, so occasionally I will convince him to have a small glass of brandy or whiskey before an auction. As a matter of fact, that's what we did. It was the Johnny Walker blue label. His favorite." His voice wavered, and there was a poignant pause as he cleared his throat. "I figured it was only appropriate this was his last one before he..." He trailed off, letting his gaze linger on the floor instead of the chief's penetrating stare. "Retired."

Angela locked eyes with Chief Helbar for a split second. *Are you thinking what I am?*

The chief furrowed his brow as he studied Conrad, who shifted uncomfortably. Something about his demeanor struck Angela as odd. He didn't seem distraught so much as unequivocally nervous.

"Conrad," Angela's voice was gentle, but firm, as she laid a hand on his shoulder. "I understand this is difficult, but anything you can tell us would be an immense amount of help. "

"Of course," Conrad muttered, his gaze still fixed on the lifeless form of his partner. When he turned to Angela, his expression was somber. "I wish I could tell you more, but honestly, I have no idea what caused this. I was out canvassing the auction floor the entire time."

Angela nodded. That much, at least, was true. She had seen it with her own eyes.

The sound of a second set of footsteps approaching echoed through the locker room. Angela turned just as Dr. Caldwell and his team arrived.

"All right, Harold, what have we got?" As the chief explained everything they knew, and Dr. Caldwell's team prepared Sterling's body for removal, Angela decided it was time to regroup and plan for their next steps.

She pulled out her phone and dialed Kim. "Hey. Dr. Caldwell is here collecting the body. I think it's safe to bring Ruff back in now. I want to take him with me when I go back onto the auction floor."

"You're going back out there?" Kim asked. "What for? Our lead has gone cold."

Angela allowed herself a smile as she made her way toward the door. "Just because we lost one lead today doesn't mean it's the only one. After all, Michelle is a reporter. Maybe she found out something we don't know."

Kim hummed. "Hmm, that's not a bad idea." A few minutes later, she breezed in, and Ruff trotted back to Angela's side with a joyful bark.

Finally, back to where the action is!

He pressed against Angela as they maneuvered away from the crime scene, leaving the chief and Kim to stay with Conrad while Officer Townsend helped Dr. Caldwell.

Chapter 5

G uests milled about in every direction as Angela and Ruff maneuvered through the crowded ballroom, their faces flushed as they clutched their purchases. All the lights were on now, but even then, she could barely see beyond the flurry of fur coats, boas, and extravagant dresses blocking her view.

"Angela!" Michelle's familiar voice broke through her confusion, and she shuffled around just in time to avoid colliding directly with her friend.

"Hey, Michelle," Angela greeted, keeping her racing thoughts at bay. A simple sting operation had just gone sour, and there were still far too many unanswered questions. "Any updates?"

"Angela, what happened?" Michelle's brows furrowed, and Angela cringed. What must she look like right now? "You look like you've seen a ghost."

"Something like that," Angela replied, forcing out a hoarse laugh, and dropping into a nearby empty chair. "The sting operation turned into a suicide investigation. I thought Sterling was trying to make a run for it, but I found him slumped over in the locker room with no pulse. The coroner just took him for an examination."

Michelle's eyes widened, and her hand flew up to cover her mouth. "Are they sure it was a suicide?"

"Can't say for sure yet," Angela admitted, glancing around to make sure no one was eavesdropping. "There was no note, but I could smell alcohol on his breath. I'd bet there were traces of it in his system. We'll have to wait for the medical examiner's report to know more." Her gaze flickered between the confused customers and Officer Dell and Townsend, who had stepped away from the crime scene to help the security staff maintain order.

Michelle patted Angela's arm before turning back to the crowd. "I'll see what else I can find out from the guests."

"Thanks, Michelle. You keep an eye on things here. I'm going to talk to Chief Helbar and see if Sterling's business partner gave us anything else useful. He came into the locker room, right when we were calling the coroner."

As she walked away with Ruff at her heels, Angela's eyes scanned the room, taking in the flurry of activity as the auction patrons argued with one another and tried to defend their purchases. Michelle remained calm amidst the chaos, her keen gaze never missing a beat as she hung on every word, acting every bit the skilled reporter she was.

Angela approached Officer Townsend, who stood nearby, corralling a small circle of people. She pulled him over to the side, away from curious onlookers and prying eyes.

"Did Conrad say anything else when the chief talked to him?" she asked.

Officer Townsend shook his head, rubbing the back of his neck. "He's pretty shaken up. Seems adamant Sterling never drank more than a drop of alcohol at a time since getting clean. "

"Clean?" Angela raised an eyebrow. What did that mean? Was the chief right about Sterling's addiction?

"Yup." Officer Townsend nodded. "Definitely something we should investigate. I'm going to check out local AA meetings and see if Sterling's registered for any lately."

"Good idea," Angela agreed. "In the meantime, I'll talk to Conrad myself. See if I can find out more."

With a nod, Officer Townsend headed back into the fray while Angela kept her eyes peeled for Conrad. She had little luck, but she ran into Michelle again. Judging from the downtrodden look on her face, Angela couldn't say she felt extremely hopeful.

"Did you find anything useful?"

Michelle pursed her lips as she peered through the notebook, which was surprisingly more than a third of the way full. "Unfortunately, no. Most of these people are clueless about the fakes. They're so determined to prove their purchases are the real thing they even tried to pull up evidence on their phone, no matter how many times I pointed out that they never received a certificate of authenticity. Anything I said only made them more upset. But I'll keep digging."

"Good," Angela said, her tone appreciative. "We'll need all the help we can get."

When they parted ways, Angela headed for the front of the hotel, stepping out into the brisk autumn air as it nipped at her cheeks. Ruff followed closely at her heels, his senses on high alert and his nose glued firmly to the ground. There had been no sign of Conrad in the auction room, and Ruff hoped they weren't too late to catch him if he did flee.

Ruff kept pace with Angela as she weaved her way through groups of chattering townsfolk who were speculating about what could be taking place in the ballroom. Angela caught a few snippets of conversation here and there. Some people thought it was a secret celebrity wedding, while others were opting for an exclusive gathering of debutants or other socialites.

Endless possibilities whirled around them, but Angela did her best to stay focused on the task ahead of them.

As they rounded a corner, she spotted Conrad leaning against the side of the hotel, looking distressed as he clutched his cell phone and pressed it to his ear.

Hmm. that's odd. Angela exchanged significant looks with Ruff, and they crept forward. She motioned for him to stay back as they hid behind a sturdy oak tree. Its gnarled bark pressed against her shoulder, but her mind was already running a million miles per hour and she barely registered the pain. Conrad's hands trembled, his Adam's apple bobbing as he whispered in harsh, hushed tones. His words echoed in the wind just loud enough for Angela to hear as he pressed himself against the brick exterior of the hotel.

"Look, I promise you'll get your money," his voice crackled with desperation and his eyes darted along the street. Angela and Ruff kept themselves hidden, just in case he had any inkling he was being watched. "This is just a small snafu, nothing we can't handle."

Angela frowned, and Ruff let out a low growl. Who was Conrad talking to? And why did he look like he thought he was about to get mugged? Better still, why did he seem more concerned about whoever was on the other end of that phone call than the fact that his business partner had just died?

A twig snapped behind her, and Angela spun around, her heart thundering against her ribcage. She let out a long breath when she realized it was Kim exiting the hotel. Conrad nearly jumped out of his skin and quickly hung up the phone call before resuming his stance, leaning against the building, and pulling out what looked like a cigar from his back pocket. Angela raised a brow. Maybe Sterling wasn't the only one with the habit he wanted to keep hidden. She beckoned Ruff to her side and did her best to look inconspicuous as they crossed the street to meet Kim near the surveillance van, which had been disguised as a delivery truck.

"Hey. The chief is looking for you. What are you doing?"

They both landed at the spot where Conrad had been leaning, only to realize that he had all but disappeared. Angela frowned. "I was looking for Conrad. I was hoping you'd be able to tell me a bit more about Sterling, since he didn't seem to give up much to the chief."

Kim placed her hand on her hip. "You know how Helbar is sometimes. He wants facts cut and dried, and he doesn't have time for any shenanigans."

Angels nodded and stifled a laugh. That was one way to put it. Abrasive was another. "True," she mused. "but when people are shaken up after witnessing their business partner die, stop breathing down their necks..."

Kim smirked. "Yeah, not the most productive way to find information."

"Exactly."

Kim's gaze drifted over to where Angela and Ruff had last seen him, and she shoved her hands in her pockets. "Oh well, it looks like you found him. Did he give you anything?"

Angela shook her head as she toyed with Ruff's leash. "Not exactly. When I caught up to him, he was on a phone call. I don't know who it was or what it was about, but he sounded pretty freaked out. Said something about promising whoever was on the other line they would get their money, and this was just a snafu."

Kim whistled. "We'll trace his cell. The chief already wants to call him in for questioning, so maybe I can have the IT department see what they can find out."

Angela nodded. "Sounds like a solid plan."

As they turned to head back inside, Conrad rounded the building. He looked even more flustered than he had before and now, pacing back and forth along the sidewalk, not saying anything as he continued his conversation on the phone.

Angela and Kim met up with the chief and agreed to meet him at the station the next morning for a breakdown. After dropping Michelle off at her office, Angela headed home to complete her daily chores around the farm. She did quick work of feeding her animals before making herself a light dinner and calling her boyfriend David. He would be home from teaching by now, and she was dying to fill him in on the case.

He picked it up after the first ring. "Hey, Angie."

"Hey, David," Angela replied as she stroked Ruff's head, which was resting in her lap. "What's up?"

"Oh, just working on a case. You know, the usual."

David laughed, a rich, hearty sound. "You're only happy when there's trouble, aren't you?"

"That's why I got into the business," Angela shot back.

"So, what is it this time?"

Angela leaned back into the couch cushions, cradling the phone between her ear and shoulder. "Remember the auctioneer we were doing a sting on because the police thought he was part of an art forgery ring?"

"Yeah…" A pause. "What about him?"

"He died today."

David gasped. "No way! Weren't you supposed to pull this thing yesterday?"

Angela nodded and brushed back her hair. "Yep. And we almost had him too. The chief was not happy."

David let out a long breath. "I bet he wasn't. Do you know what happened?"

Angela shifted. "We thought it was a suicide at first, but now it looks like poisoning."

"Poisoning? Who would do that?"

Angela shrugged. "Not sure yet. But the auction had quite a few unhappy customers. You wanna know something crazy?"

David chuckled ruefully. "Don't I always?"

Angela smiled. "Victor was there."

"Victor? As in Victor Callahan?" David's voice rose, and Angela could practically picture his eyebrows rising into his hairline.

"Yep." Angela nodded, swallowing an incredulous laugh. "He was after an epergne for a customer, which somehow wound up with Sterling."

"Was it real?"

Angela crossed her legs. "Victor seemed pretty positive."

"And? Did he get it?"

Angela's lips curled into a smile. "He did. Bid an arm and a leg, though."

David whistled softly. "Well, at least his customer will be happy. What's your next move?"

"I'm calling the auction house tomorrow." Angela leaned forward. "I want to see if they have anything useful in their records."

"Make it after school," David said. "I'm coming with you."

Angela's smile widened even as she rolled her eyes. "I don't need a chaperone, David."

He laughed. "Last time you went solo, you nearly got yourself poisoned. So, I'm coming. No arguments."

Angela chuckled, her heart warmed by his insistence. "Alright, I'll try for an appointment after 3p.m."

"Thank you." Relief coated David's words, and Angela melted.

"Of course. Love you."

"Love you too."

Chapter 6

A ngela pulled into the parking lot and maneuvered into the spot closest to the door. When she walked inside and made her way to Kim's desk, she found Officer Townsend already seated next to Kim in a plush leather rolling chair. They started combing through the public record of the auction house page after page, but nothing seemed to be out of order.

Frustration gnawed at Angela as they drove down one rabbit hole after another, only to find a tangled web of dummy shell corporations.

"Dead end after dead end," Kim muttered, rubbing her temples. "Whoever's behind this is good."

"Too good," Officer Townsend agreed.

Kim let out a long sigh as she exited out of the many tabs open on her computer. She leaned against the back of her chair, running both hands down her face. Angela squeezed her shoulder.

"Don't worry, we'll figure this out. We've only been investigating for a couple of hours."

Of course we will, Ruff barked in agreement as he ambled over to lick the hand that was hanging down at Kim's side. She flashed him a weary smile, followed by a rewarding pat on the head which made him growl contentedly.

"Thanks, you guys." Kim removed her police cap and let her natural hair out. "I know it has only been a couple of days, but we've been trying to catch these guys since your dad was on the force. I just wanna lock them down, you know?"

Angela nodded and her mind drifted back to the file folder that was still in the front console of her car. She hadn't had time to examine it yet. Maybe now would be the perfect opportunity.

But before she could even put words to the thought, Chief Helbar burst into the room, his face flushed and eyes a half shade darker than usual. Officer Townsend and Kim both jumped to their feet. "What is it, chief?" she asked.

"Yeah," Officer Townend echoed. "What's going on?"

He sat down in the chair across from Kim's desk and gave them all a serious look. "I just got off the phone with the coroner. Preliminary autopsy report came in. There were traces of Strychnine in Sterling's blood."

"Poison?" Angela's heart clenched. Strychnine was a chemical that used to be common in old Western-style salons. People thought it had curative properties, diluting it into bourbon or whiskey even when they found out it was poison, because the drink was still safer to drink than many of the tap water supplies back then. Nowadays, though, a small dose could be lethal and cause excruciating muscle spasms before lactic acidosis or other equally unpleasant illnesses set in.

The chief nodded. "The effort to procure it would indicate that it was premeditated. Makes little sense that Sterling would ingest it before such a big event. Seems our man didn't take his own life after all."

Angela exchanged a somber glance with Kim as the chief began barked orders. "Officer Dell, keep digging into those financial records. The skeletons we're looking for are in that closet for sure."

"Will do, Chief," Kim replied, nodding resolutely, already turning back to the computer.

"Angela," Chief Helbar barked. She met his gaze with a steady one of her own. "At your service, Chief."

Ruff barked, puffing out his chest as the chief nodded. "Can you and Ruff go to the auction house? We may not find much online, but you might dig up something from their paper records."

"On it," Angela replied as she pushed to her feet. "And I'll see if my father knows anything, too. This used to be his case, after all."

The chief nodded resolutely and gave them a faint smile. "You do that and say hi to Charlie and your mother for me. How is she doing, by the way?"

Angela smiled as she rounded the desk and stood in the aisle of the station. "Much better. Her burns healed nicely, and she hasn't had an episode since then."

About a week prior to Thanksgiving, Angela's mother Abigail had accidentally burned herself trying to cook a Thanksgiving turkey. She had early onset dementia, and could sometimes get dates mixed up. That day, Abigail was convinced it was going to be Thanksgiving in a matter of hours, and was determined to make the perfect turkey before she had an accident. She ended up needing a trip to the ER, but thankfully the doctors could heal her burns without too much medical intervention.

Chief Helbar broke into a smile as the lines around his eyes crinkled. "I'm glad to hear that." He placed a heavy but gentle hand on Angela's shoulder and squeezed it tightly before walking off. "Good luck, everyone."

Angela exchanged rueful smiles with the rest of the police staff as she prepared to leave the station.

"Well, duty calls."

Kim waved and gave her an encouraging wink. "Let's hope you have better luck than we did."

Angela laughed as Ruff lumbered to her side. "I'll keep you posted."

Chapter 7

Angela sat at her cluttered desk as Ruff lay contentedly at her feet. When she had first bought her office, one of her first purchases had been a dog bed, but Ruff scarcely used it anymore. He preferred to take his afternoon naps either on the couch that sat near the door of her office or beneath her desk. It took a bit of searching, but Angela eventually located the number for the auction house and rang them up.

"Hummings Hollow Auction House. How may I assist you?" a polite voice echoed through the speaker after the second ring.

"Hello, this is Angela Atkinson. I am a private detective working with the Hummings Hollow police on a recent investigation."

"There was a brief pause on the line before the voice responded. "Hi, Angela. I'm Kelly. How can we help you?"

"Unfortunately, I'm calling regarding one of your former auctioneers. He was pronounced dead earlier this morning, and we believe he may have been murdered."

Kelly gasped. "Oh my, that's horrible."

"It is," Angela agreed. "But to determine what happened, I need access to your records for that auction, including sales records, item descriptions, and bidder lists. I have a warrant."

Kelly clicked her tongue. "I see. Well, we take these matters seriously. Could you come in tomorrow around 4p.m?"

Angela nodded and scribbled a note on her calendar. "That sounds good. In the meantime, I'll email you a copy of the warrant just so you have it for your records. And I assure you the identities of the bidders and sellers will remain private."

"We appreciate your cooperation as well," Kelly said through the receiver. "I'll inform my manager, and we will see you tomorrow."

After exchanging contact information, Angela sent off the warrant and crossed her fingers. Hopefully, the visit tomorrow would be a lucrative one.

The next day, Angela parked her car in front of the auction house and got out with David, Ruff bounding quickly after them. He was wearing his vest again, though thankfully this time he didn't put up much of a fight. Angela took a deep breath, arching her back in a cat stretch as the crisp air filled her lungs. Then she opened her wallet and took out the warrant Officer Jeffrey had been so quick to procure for her.

When they entered the elegant building, a receptionist greeted them and directed them to a small office at the back. The secretary, a middle-aged woman, welcomed Angela with a warm smile. "Angela, I'm Kelly. We spoke on the phone."

Angela nodded and held out her hand. "Hi Kelly, I'm Angela, and this is my... partner, David."

David pushed his glasses up on his nose and waved. "Nice to meet you."

"You as well," Kelly replied. "Though I must say I wish it was under better circumstances."

Angela gave her a sympathetic smile. "Believe me, we wish the same."

Kelly nodded and gestured to the seats. "Please, have a seat. I'll fetch the records for you."

Angela and David thanked her and settled into the plush chair, Ruff at their side. The aroma of old books and antique furniture tinged the air in the room, and the soft hum of the air conditioning whirred in the background.

Kelly returned a few minutes later with a stack of folders and documents. "Here you go. These are all the records you requested. If you need anything else or have questions, please don't hesitate to ask."

Angela nodded as she took the documents and split it between her and David. "Thank you, Kelly. If I find anything relevant, I'll be sure to let you know."

One by one, they began flipping through the stacks of paper. At first, Angela nor David saw anything out of the ordinary, but then–

"Look at this." Angela pulled a paper out of the stack and handed it to David. He leaned forward, craning his neck to inspect the document. It was an order form with a list of items in the latest auction. Some seemed legitimate, but a noticeable number of the alleged forgeries were missing.

David furrowed his brows as he examined it. "I don't get it," he said. "What am I looking at?"

Angela leaned closer to him, trailing a finger along the item lines. "It's what you are not looking at. Victor was convinced most of the items were forgeries, and it looks like they aren't listed here."

David nodded, rubbing his chin as he adjusted his glasses. "So, Victor was onto something."

Angela glanced at the statement again. "Exactly. And you know Victor, always meticulous with his stock."

David scratched his head. "That epergne is one of the few things listed here. We should find out more about Victor's customer and why they are so interested in it."

Angela hesitated for a moment, then let out a long breath. "You're right, David. But, you know, we've investigated him before. It's like walking on broken glass now. Besides, I'm sure Victor would have checked the backgrounds of the customers he dealt with. The last thing he would want is to entangle himself with any of this." She gestured to the papers and David nodded.

"That's true," he agreed. "But you said we should follow every lead. This is one of them."

Angela sighed, running a hand through her hair. "Okay, we'll look into it. First, I want to see Sterling's office."

David hummed and inched toward the door. "Let's go find Kelly and see if she can show us where it is."

They stepped across the hallway to Kelly's office, lingering in the doorway before they entered. Angela poked her head in and cleared her throat as Kelly looked up from where she was typing away on her computer. "Hi again, Kelly. My partner and I were wondering... is there any way we could see Sterling's office?"

Kelly smiled, pushing her chair back from her desk. "Of course. Follow me."

The woman led them to a small office tucked away in the back of the building, behind an unassuming gray door. "Everything should be in here."

"Thanks," Angela replied as she ducked into the room with Ruff and David trailing behind her.

Hours passed as Angela and David meticulously combed through Sterling's bank statements. Her eyes widened as she noticed a series of large, unexplained payments to an unknown account dating back several months.

"David, I think I found something," she whispered. Ruff barked in agreement, even though he wasn't entirely sure what he was agreeing to.

"What have you got?" David cleaned his glasses with the rag he always kept in the pocket of his sweater vest, and Angela smiled. When they had first been on a blind date set up by her niece Megan, Angela had thought his sense of style was questionable. But over time, she grew to not only appreciate it, but to find it to be one of the many quirky things she loved about him.

"I wonder where this money is going?" David wondered as he skimmed the documents.

Angela leaned closer. As she studied the transactions more closely, she scrutinized every number in line for some clue as to the true destination of the funds, but found nothing. Still, she took a picture of the documents on her phone and texted them to Kim.

Try searching these account numbers.

Angela pocketed the phone, and they continued their search. Papers and antique curiosities were everywhere, but even after searching every nook and cranny, they were still coming up empty.

They were just about to leave, but a small squirrel perched on a tree branch outside the window caught Ruff's eye. He bounded around the room, bumping into the leg of the polished desk.

"Ruff, Stop!" Angela scrambled to grab his leash, her eyes darting to the door, and she breathed a sigh of relief when there was no sound of high heels clapping against the tile. Maybe Kelly hadn't heard them after all.

Ruff won the tug-of-war contest, but settled down as soon as Angela dragged him away from the window and his intended prey. "I know you're excited, boy, but you've got to stay calm. We can't get caught messing around in here."

Look what I found.

Angela's mouth dropped open when a small click resonated through the room.

"What was that?"

She squinted and her eyes widened when she caught sight of a small hidden indentation of a hummingbird in the intricate carvings on one of the desk's legs. It was a rounded circle that protruded a little more than the rest of the design carved into the wood. It looked like it had been halfway pushed in and Angela pushed it all the way open. The side of the display slid away to reveal a secret compartment filled to the brim with old, yellowing envelopes. Ruff's eyes almost welled with curiosity.

"David, look what Ruff found!" Angela exclaimed as she gingerly removed the dusty envelopes from the compartment.

David spun around from where he was hovering near the other side of the office. "What have you got—Whoa." he hurried to her side as she delicately pinched one envelope between her fingers. The seal on it practically fell apart as she tore it open and unfolded the letter, skimming the first few paragraphs. It was from one of Sterling's disgruntled clients. He was demanding a refund and claiming that if he didn't get one within a week with some form of compensation, he was going to turn in his counterfeit purchase to the police. Chief Helbar never said anything about receiving any counterfeit pieces, So Angela assumed Sterling had reimbursed him.

As she sifted through the pile of correspondence that cluttered the corner of her desk, she noticed a particularly crisp envelope. Unlike the others, it was not yellowed with age, indicating its recent arrival. The sender's address caught her eye: Valentina Balducci. The date stamped on the envelope was just two weeks prior.

When she peeled it open, her eyes widened. The letter was written in a neat, albeit agitated, handwriting.

Dear Mr. Hastings,

I came to your auction because I thought at long last, I had finally found my grandmother's epergne. The last glass piece she ever made. The piece I went home with, however, was nothing more than a cheap imitation.

I want my money back, Sterling. Every single penny. And trust me, if you try to weasel your way out of this, I won't hesitate to go to the police.

Valentina Balducci

As Angela and David continued sifting through the documents, they noticed seven more envelopes bearing Valentina Balducci's name and address.

David turned back to the letters, his brows furrowing. "Did Sterling ever respond to any of these? If he was involved in any of the forgery rings, maybe he made her some promises to keep her quiet."

"Promises he couldn't keep, evidently," Angela added.

She scanned the room, heading over to the trash bin as a hunch. Sure enough, beneath several other couple pieces of paper, was indeed a letter to Valentina. Sterling was practically begging her to stay quiet, saying he knew what would happen if she opened her mouth.

David and Angela exchanged a knowing look.

"We need to meet with Valentina," David said. "Find out everything she knows about Sterling's deals."

Angela nodded. "Agreed. I'll go first thing tomorrow."

After another few minutes of searching with no other discoveries, they stepped out of the office with the bank statements in hand. "Thank you, Kelly. I think we have everything we need for now. I'll let you know if I need to come back."

"Of course, Angela," Kelly replied. "Come back anytime you need."

They bid her goodbye and made it out to the car, a million thoughts swirling around in Angela's mind.

Chapter 8

R *ing, Ring! Ring, Ring!*

Angela moaned and rolled over, burying her head under her pillow as her cell phone rang incessantly on her nightstand. Most nights, she tried to remember to keep it silent for this very reason.

Who on earth could that be?

Ruff growled from his spot, curled up on the edge of her bed, glaring at the incessantly vibrating metal rectangle as it bounced its way toward the end of Angela's night table. Maybe if he let it fall, he could step on it, and then that ringing would stop.

When the phone rang for the fourth time, he decided to act on it. But before he could reach it to nudge it off, Angela reached out and grabbed the phone.

Groggily, she picked it up, squinting at the caller ID through bleary eyes crusted with sleep.

"What—Victor?" she muttered.

Ruff tilted his head to the side. *Why would Mr. Callahan be calling at—he glanced at the clock—at 3:30a.m. in the morning?*

Angela frowned as the antique shop owner's name flashed on the screen. Sighing, she picked it up, answering just before the fifth ring could finish. "Hello?" Angela mumbled. Her voice was thick with sleep, and at this point, she wasn't even awake enough to discern whether it was intelligible

"Angela!" Victor's shout echoed in her ear, and she yanked the receiver away from her face. Well, now she was wide awake. "Finally! What took you so long?"

Angela moaned as she pushed up into a sitting position and rubbed her eyes. "Victor? Why are you calling me at this unearthly time?"

A loud sigh echoed on the other end of the line. "Keep up, Miss Atkinson. I finally got the one piece I've been searching for, and now I can't even sell it to my most loyal customer! She's been looking for it her whole life, and it's ruined mine! What am I going to do? Better yet, what are you going to do for me?"

"Wait, slow down," Angela interrupted. "What the heck are you talking about, Victor? It's the middle of the night."

"Did you not hear anything I said?" he sputtered. "Someone has robbed my shop!"

"Victor, why didn't you just call 911 first?" Angela asked, exhaustion seeping into her words.

"I did," he grumbled. "But they're too slow. You've got connections with Chief Helbar, and I know you can get them moving faster."

Angela rolled his eyes. Retorts danced on the edge of her tongue, but she held them back and sighed; arguing with him would only waste time. If there really was a break-in, they had to get there as quickly as possible.

"Alright, alright," Angela sighed, doing her best to suppress the annoyance bubbling up within her. "Stay put, Victor. I'll call Chief Helbar, and we'll be there as soon as we can."

"Make it quick!" he snapped before a dial tone resounded in her ear.

"Great," Angela muttered under her breath as she dialed Chief Helbar's number. He was notoriously irritable when it came to being woken up, and she braced herself for an inevitable earful when she revealed the source of their disturbance. Ruff sat up beside her, nuzzling against her leg.

"Helbar here," grumbled the gruff voice on the other end of the line after the third ring.

"Chief, it's Angela. Victor Callahan just called me saying someone robbed his shop. He wants us down there right away."

"Of course he does," Chief Helbar grumbled. "Alright, I'll meet you there. Just give me a few minutes to get dressed."

"See you soon," Angela replied before hanging up. She swung her legs over the side of the bed, her feet finding the familiar comfort of her slippers, and glanced at Ruff. "Well, boy, you know what they say, a detective's work is never done," she said as she grabbed her keys and headed for the door.

Ruff grunted. *And it seems neither is a dog's work.* He gave a large stretch and then reluctantly followed Angela. She threw on some clothes and brushed her teeth before grabbing her keys and heading out the door.

As Angela drove through the quiet streets of Hummings Hollow, she sighed. In a small town, everyone knew everyone else's business. Most of the time she loved that about Hummings Hollow, but times like tonight were both comforting and frustrating, especially when anyone could ask anything of you at any time.

"Next time," she mused, spinning around to smile at Ruff in the backseat as she parked near Victor's shop. "I'm turning my phone off for the night."

Ruff barked, then nodded resolutely. That sounded like a great idea to him.

She cut the engine, opened the car door, and stepped out into the chilly night air. Ruff bounded down beside her as she spotted Chief Helbar.

Angela and Ruff approached the door with Chief Helbar close behind. The faint sound of wind chimes filled the air. Even in the dim light, Angela couldn't help but appreciate the charm of the old building, enhanced by the fact that Victor loved it enough to do his best to keep it in good shape. Which, come to think of it, must be why the apparent break-in had him so rattled.

"Victor really should have waited for us," she muttered when she reached the door, only to test the handle and find it locked.

"Couldn't agree more," grumbled Chief Helbar. "But you know Victor. With him, it always must be his way or the highway." The chief rolled his eyes, and Angela stifled a smile. That sounded a lot like someone else she knew. Not that she would ever say that out loud.

Angela tried again, and this time, the door relented. She cautiously pushed it open, startled when a shrill alarm pierced the night air.

Ruff's ears perked up, his body tense and ready to protect Angela at any cost.

"What the heck is that?" Angela yelled, cringing as she clapped her hand over her ears to block out at least some of the sound.

"Oh, great!" The chief shouted back. "I think Victor finally took our advice and installed that stupid alarm system. Guess that explains how he knew there was a break-in!"

Before Angela could reply, Victor Callahan appeared at the top of the staircase, his face flushed with an ironic mix of panic and indignation.

"Would've been nice if you called before barging in!" he snapped, hurrying down the steps and punching the code in on the keypad to silence the alarm. "You could've warned me!"

"Likewise, Victor," Angela retorted, rubbing her temples as the last echoes of the ringing faded away. "Now that we're all here, let's see what the damage is."

Chief Helbar grunted, and the three of them set about examining the shop. As they navigated through the clutter, Angela felt a pang of sympathy for Victor. Despite his theatrics, he had poured his heart and soul into this place. Papers were scattered everywhere. Books had been knocked over, and even a few of the glass curio cases had been broken, though nothing appeared to be taken from them.

"Any idea who might've done this?" she asked Victor as he gingerly led them around the damaged areas.

"None," he replied bitterly. "Apart from that blasted auction, I've always been careful with my dealings." He pressed his lips together and ran a hand through his hair. "I know I'm not everyone's cup of tea in this town, but I can't think of anyone who would want to hurt me like this."

Angela lay a hand on his shoulder. He was right: he was far from her favorite, but no one deserved to be robbed.

"Let's just focus on finding clues for now," Chief Helbar interjected, the extra layer of hoarseness in his voice betraying his exhaustion. "We can speculate later."

Angela surveyed the wreckage while Ruff stood protectively by her side, his ears perked and nose twitching, as if waiting for the moment when the intruder might return.

"Unbelievable," Chief Helbar muttered, shaking his head. They had been searching for nearly half an hour and found no evidence of anything missing. "They trashed the place but didn't take a single thing? What kind of burglar does that?"

Victor's face was ashen, his eyes wide. "it is quite odd," he agreed, "Especially since I just acquired an extremely valuable piece from an auction. Why would they go to all this trouble and not take it?" He gestured helplessly at the epergne, which, despite a thorough examination, appeared to be entirely intact.

Angela sighed, wishing she had answers for him. "I'm so sorry, Victor. But I can assure you, we'll do everything we can to find out who did this."

"Thank you, Angela," Victor said, managing a small, grateful smile. "I know I can count on you."

Chief Helbar scratched his stubbled chin. "We'll need to review your security footage. Maybe it'll give us some clues as to what they were after."

"And why they didn't get it," Angela added.

"Of course," Victor agreed, as the determined glint in his eye returned. "Whatever it takes to catch these criminals."

As they made their way to the back room where he kept the security system, Ruff whined softly.

Angela glanced around the trashed shop once more, her eyes lingering on the mess, before turning to Victor. "You know, maybe your new security system is actually doing its job," she mused with a small laugh. "After that whole rare cookbook fiasco, it seems like it's keeping thieves from getting away with anything valuable."

Victor frowned, clearly not amused. He crossed his arms and huffed indignantly. "Well, it obviously didn't stop them from making a complete mess of my store!"

Angela nodded but allowed a small chuckle to escape at her own joke, earning glares from both Victor and Chief Helbar.

They made it into the security room, and Victor pulled up the footage from the last three hours, which the chief said was plenty of time to examine the possible break-in. As it was nearly 4a.m. though, he made a compromise that they would tend to it first thing tomorrow morning.

When Victor didn't agree immediately, the chief cleared his throat and ushered Angela forward. "We appreciate your cooperation, Victor," he said with finality as he shoved the front door open and ushered Angela out into the night.

Chapter 9

The next morning, Angela arrived at the police station with Ruff in tow, ready to analyze the security footage from Victor's shop. She hoped it would provide some leads on the perpetrator, but as she sat down with Chief Helbar to review the tape, she quickly realized it wouldn't be so easy.

"Darn it," she muttered under her breath. Her eyes never left the screen as an unidentifiable figure in black moved through the shop. They kept their face turned away from the cameras, making them nearly impossible to identify. The only discernible feature was a pair of piercing blue eyes, visible for just a fraction of a second as they glanced up at one camera.

"Looks like we're dealing with a professional, or at least someone who knows what they're doing," Chief Helbar said gruffly, stroking his chin.

"Blue eyes aren't much to go on," Angela admitted. "But the perpetrator's build suggests a male."

"True," the chief agreed. "We'll have to keep digging. In the meantime, we should keep an eye on other businesses in town. If this guy was after something specific in Victor's shop, he might try another place."

Angela nodded, her mind racing. What could the thief have been looking for in Victor's shop? Last night she would've put all her money into the epergne, but out of everything in the shop, it had seemed the most untouched. Even if they didn't get exactly what they wanted, why would they leave without taking a single thing? It was a lot of trouble to go through without reaping a reward.

That afternoon, Angela returned to her PI office, where a stack of auction house records awaited her. She sank into her chair and began leafing through the papers. Ruff lay by her feet, napping contentedly. Angela smiled to herself as his soft snores echoed through the office.

"Angela!" When she was half a stack of papers deep, a familiar voice called from the doorway, startling her. Kathy, an old coworker of hers from the Lake House coffee shop, leaned against the door frame with a takeout bag in hand. "Did you forget about our lunch date?"

"Kathy!" Angela exclaimed. She sprang to her feet as her cheeks flushed. "Oh my gosh, I completely forgot! I'm so sorry. Please, come in."

She glanced at the clock. It was nearly 1:30. No wonder her stomach had been growling for the past hour.

As Kathy entered, Angela noticed how much her friend had grown since they'd last seen each other. They made small talk and pride swelled in Angela's chest as Kathy shared her most recent accomplishments.

"I'm doing well," she said, grinning. "I'm even thinking of going into forensics like you as a long-term career when the dust settles."

"Forensics, huh?" Angela teased. "Are you sure you want to spend your days combing through crime scenes and analyzing evidence? It's not as glamorous as it looks on TV."

"Definitely," Kathy replied. Her eyes sparkled as she leaned forward and glanced at the stack of papers Angela had pushed to the side to make room for them to have lunch. "I've always admired your dedication. Whatever I do, I know I want to make a difference, like you."

Angela smiled. "Aw, you're too sweet."

Kathy laughed and cut a hand through the air before pulling her burger from the takeout bag. Ruff was instantly drawn to the tantalizing scent of meat, drool dripping off the side of his mouth.

Yum! And I thought she didn't bring me a treat today. Usually, they stopped at the Lake House a lot more frequently than they had been lately. Ruff never passed up the opportunity for Kathy to squirt some cream on his nose, which she always did whenever she thought Angela wasn't looking.

He leaped toward the delicious-smelling food, soaring over Angela's computer monitor and scattering the stack of auction house papers that sat precariously on the corner of Angela's desk.

"Ruff!" Angela scolded as the papers fluttered across the office floor. "You need to be more careful!"

"Sorry about that," Kathy said with a chuckle. "He just couldn't resist the smell of fresh food."

She tore off a piece of her burger, and Ruff stood on his hind legs as he carefully took it between his lips, chewing slowly and trying to savor it.

Angela shook her head and laughed ruefully. "You're a ham, you know that?"

Ruff shrugged. *Maybe I am, but you love me anyway.*

"Here, let me help you with these," Kathy offered.

Angela shook her head. "Don't worry about it." Her voice softened as she patted Ruff's head before bending down to help her collect the rest of the papers. "It was an accident. Ruff was due a treat, anyway."

She winked at him, and he grinned.

Don't I always?

"Besides," Angela added with a mischievous glint in her eye, "nothing can keep me from solving this case. Not even a hungry border collie."

They laughed. As they picked up the documents, Angela scrutinized one page more closely, her brow furrowing in confusion. "There's a discrepancy in the auction records."

Her eyes grew wider the longer she tried to piece it together. This wasn't just a slight discrepancy like the one before, and it couldn't even be attributed to a lost item. As if she needed any more proof that this wasn't Sterling's first rodeo with the forgery ring. Well, she had it right here.

Just as they were finishing lunch, Angela's phone rang. She turned it over on her desk and then groaned upon recognizing Victor Callahan's name on the caller ID. She sighed, bracing herself as she hit ACCEPT on the second ring.

"Victor, what is it this time?" She asked.

"Remember that customer I was telling you about? She just came by," Victor huffed. "She's studied epergnes for years and thinks that the piece I have is a fake! I swear, Angela, I bought the real one at the auction."

"I'll be right there," Angela promised, hanging up the phone with a sigh even as her pulse picked up. She turned to Kathy. "I need to go check this out, but thank you for dropping by today. If you decide to take that forensics class, let me know."

Kathy smiled. "Will do. Be careful out there, okay?"

"Always," Angela assured her, grabbing her coat and heading out with Ruff at her side.

As they approached Victor's store, Angela's mind whirled. What if the auctions were just the tip of the iceberg in a much larger conspiracy?

The scent of old wood and dust mingled with the faintest hint of lavender.

"Victor, are you here?" Angela called out, scanning the dimly lit store. Her gaze settled on Chief Helbar near the back, examining the fake epergne with a frown on his weathered face.

"I'm here. Victor grumbled. "And so is my customer, Valentina. She's over there having a right fit about this, not that I blame her."

Angela raised an eyebrow as he pointed toward a woman with raven hair, sharp features, light skin, and fiery eyes. Could she be Valentina Balducci, the woman who was dealing with Sterling too? Valentina glared at the counterfeit piece displayed on a pedestal. At the sound of newcomers, her gaze darted toward Angela's. She could practically feel the heat radiating from her. "I can't believe Sterling had the audacity to sell me this... this trash!"

Angela pressed her lips together and marched resolutely toward the back of the store, stepping up next to the chief. "What's going on?"

The chief grumbled and crossed his arms. "Well, I'm sure Victor already told you he's pretty sure this epergne is a fake. We're gonna have to get someone from the station down here to verify for sure, though."

Angela frowned as her gaze darted helplessly between the antique and Victor's distracted customer. The piece looked rather exquisite, carved with expert hands and attention to the most minute of details. At least to the untrained eye. For someone who had been searching for this her entire life, though, it clearly didn't measure up.

She glanced at Valentina, who stood a short distance away with her arms wrapped tightly around herself. Her eyes were red-rimmed and bloodshot, but they burned with fury as she struggled to keep her composure. Angela's gaze lingered before she turned to the chief and let out a long breath. "What do we know about her?"

Chief Helbar shrugged as he stroked the ends of his mustache. "Honestly? Not much. She's one of Victor's regulars, been chasing this artifact for most of her life. Says it's a family heirloom. Her grandmother was a renowned glassblower; this piece, or the authentic one, was the last one she ever made."

Angela hummed and nodded solemnly, squeezing the chief's shoulder as she brushed past him. "Right. Well, I'm gonna go talk to her and see what I can do."

The chief snorted and leveled their gazes. "You can try," he muttered. "But don't say I didn't warn you."

Angela's brow furrowed as she paddled over to Valentina with Ruff at her side and lay a gentle hand on her shoulder.

"Valentina, hi, I'm—"

"Don't touch me!" Valentina snapped, jerking away from Angela's touch.

"I understand you're upset." Angela held her hands up in surrender, but paid no mind to the other woman's flaring temper. "But we'll sort this out, I promise. I'm just here to help."

"Upset? That's an understatement!" Valentina gestured wildly toward the epergne, pacing the length of the front of the shop. "I've invested so much in Sterling's auctions, only to be repaid with lies and deceit! And who are you, anyway?"

Angela flushed and stepped back, sticking out her hand and clearing her throat. "As I was saying before, my name is Angela Atkinson. I'm a private investigator. Victor has me here working on your case."

Valentina snorted. "A little late to call in reinforcements, isn't it, Victor?"

Victor's jaw dropped. Angela opened her mouth, but before either of them could say anything more, Valentina stormed past Angela, her heels clicking angrily against the wooden floor.

"You know what? I don't need your help." Angela winced at the disdain in her voice as she turned her icy glare to Victor. "I should have known better than to come here. They always say, if you want something done right, you must do it yourself."

Angela exchanged a pained look with Victor and the chief before scurrying after her.

"Wait, Valentina," Angela said as she caught up with her just outside the shop. Ruff stayed close, only sprinting a few paces ahead when he had to cut her off.

"Get out of my way, you mangy mutt!" She shooed Ruff away, and he growled.

Excuse me?

Angela hurried to grab a hold of him before either of them could make the situation any worse than it already was.

"Please," she panted. "Let me help you. We can work together to expose Sterling and whoever else is behind this to make sure no one else falls victim to his schemes."

Valentina hesitated, her gaze softening as she considered Angela's outstretched hand. "Alright," she agreed, clasping it in an a firm grip that nearly made Angela cringe. "But only because I want justice for the people he's deceived."

"Deal," Angela said. "Now why don't we sit down for some coffee, and you can tell me what you know."

Chapter 10

Angela exhaled slowly as she stepped into the confines of the Lake House, the coffee shop where she had spent a lot of her time before becoming a private investigator. The familiar scent of coffee mingled with fresh pastries almost made her drool. Ruff eyed Kathy, who was working behind the counter, but Angela pulled him away and toward a small quiet table in the corner where she dropped into the seat across from Valentina.

"Thanks for agreeing to talk to me."

Valentina, stirring her espresso, looked up with a guarded expression. "I just hope you were serious about letting me help you catch him. I've been chasing after Sterling for years, trying to find my grandmother's epergne. He swore to me he had it. And now that I know he didn't, I want nothing more than to see him behind bars." Valentina placed her spoon down with a clatter and leaned forward.

Angela moved closer, keeping her voice low. "I've been digging deeper into the fake antiques. We think he may be in a much larger game, a forgery ring, but we don't have any solid proof. We were at the auction a few days ago because we were trying to catch him out. Hoping if we offered him witness protection, he would act as a whistleblower."

Valentina scoffed, rolling her eyes. "Good luck with that. If there's one thing I know about Sterling, it's that he's only ever looked out for himself, unless it has some advantage for him. He will not help you."

Angela pressed her lips together. She couldn't help but notice how Valentina referred to Sterling in the present tense. Maybe she didn't know what had transpired at the auction. She opened her mouth, contemplating bringing it up, but then closed it. She needed as much information as she could get. And who knows what Valentina would do when she found out he was no longer alive?

"What else can you tell me about him?" Angela glanced around the coffee shop but was relieved to find it was mostly empty.

Valentina's eyes flashed. "Sterling's deceit cost me dearly." Valentina's grip around her cup tightened and her knuckles went white. "I've tried to call him out about it several times, but he never responded to any of my letters."

Angela hummed. That tracked with what she had found in Sterling's office. "Valentina, I hate to ask this, but... Where were you the night Sterling died?"

Valentina's eyes widened and her cheeks paled. "He's... He's dead?" She drummed her fingers against the table, taking in several shallow breaths.

"I'm afraid so," Angela replied. "Are you sure you know nothing about it?"

Valentina shook her head. "I–no, nothing. I was supposed to go to the auction, but I couldn't make it. My daughter was sick. I couldn't leave her. I sent Victor in my place." Valentina's expression softened at the mention of her daughter.

"Victor got the epergne for you," Angela informed her as she reached for a pastry.

Valentina's face lit up for half an instant before clouding over again as she stared into the depths of her coffee cup. "I know the one in the store was fake, but he swears to me on everything he owns that the one he bought was real." She relaxed a bit, a small smile playing on her lips.

"I trust him," she mumbled. "He knows how much having one of my grandmother's treasures means to me. He wouldn't tell me it was true if he wasn't certain." Angela nodded but frowned when she looked down at the floor. "I just wish I knew what happened to the real one."

"Anything you can tell me about Sterling's other dealings?" Angela pressed gently. "Anything you can tell us might help us find the answers you're looking for."

Valentina sighed. "His network was always... evasive. I know they were extensive, but I don't know how big, as I never had any personal dealings with him. I only know of him through his auctions and because I've bid so many times." She turned up her palms. "I'm sorry, but that's all I can tell you."

Her gaze shifted and her fingers clenched a little tighter around her now-empty coffee cup, but she pushed to her feet. "I would stay longer, but I must go pick up my daughter. Let me know if you need anything else."

Angela watched her closely as she made her way toward the exit, but waved her off with what she hoped was a friendly smile. "it's no problem, I understand. Enjoy the rest of your day. And thank you again for taking the time to talk to me."

As the door closed behind her, Angela pondered over their interaction. She still wasn't entirely sure that she could trust Valentina, but Victor did, and he was always good at reading people. For now, she would until Valentina gave her a reason not to.

A few hours later, she sat hunched over her desk, the dim light of the lamp highlighting the deep furrow in her brow. Her fingers traced a labyrinthine trail of financial records, her eyes following the numbers, all pointing to a web of shell corporations and tangled transactions she could only hope to decipher.

"Conrad," she muttered as his name surfaced for the fifth time in the last hour and a half. The more she delved into Sterling's finances, the clearer Conrad's involvement became. Unexplained wealth, and suspicious transactions - all red flags. And if she squinted, hints of a gambling addiction simmered just beneath the surface. She needed to talk to him, and soon. If only she knew how to find him.

As Angela sifted through the mountain of documents, one name caught her eye: Penelope Beddington. A shiver ran down her spine. Why did that sound so familiar? Angela pulled open her drawer for a fresh notepad and scribbled the name onto a scrap of paper, making a mental note to ask her father about it later. He knew this case better than almost anyone, so if anyone knew who she was, he would.

"Ruff, it's time to go home," she said softly when the light had all but disappeared from the sky outside. Angela arched her back into a cat stretch and rubbed her tired eyes. The border collie, who had been lying patiently by her feet, perked up at the sound of her voice. Angela gathered her things, shut off the desk lamp, and locked her office door behind her as she and Ruff stepped out into the cool night air.

The streetlights cast long shadows across Hummings Hollow. As Angela walked towards her car, the hair on the back of her neck stood up. She couldn't pinpoint exactly why, but she had the strange feeling she was being watched. She glanced around, her heart crawling into her throat as she looked in every direction. Ruff sensed it, too. His hackles raised, and he growled at a small patch of nearby trees. A sudden wave of fear stole her breath as she thought she saw a flicker of movement.

"Who's there?" Angela demanded, her voice steady despite the trepidation churning in her gut. Ruff hunkered himself down at her side, teeth bared as he stared into the darkness. If anyone thought they were going to get to Angela without a fight, they were very wrong.

But just as quickly as it had appeared, whoever or whatever it was vanished, leaving Angela with nothing but a sense of foreboding that chilled her to the bone. With a shudder, she hurried to her car, Ruff close on her heels, as they climbed inside.

"Stay close, Ruff," Angela whispered as she turned her key in the ignition and she headed home. She decided to take the long way for peace of mind. Her cases had been filled with danger, but she couldn't remember the last time she felt like she was being followed. It was an eerie, unsettling feeling. One she hoped she would never have to repeat anytime soon.

The early morning sunlight filtered through the thin curtains of Angela's living room, casting an eerie glow on the cluttered coffee table laden with case files and notes. She was still getting nowhere with these files, and it would be immensely helpful to have a fresh set of eyes.

Just as she leaned into the couch cushions and began drifting off with haunting images of the shadowy figure dancing in her head, her phone buzzed, jolting her from her thoughts. "Hey, Kim. What have you got for me?"

"Angela, someone from the station went down to Victor's shop and tested the antique," Kim said. "They confirmed it was a fake."

A knot formed in Angela's stomach. "Thanks, Kim. I'll handle it from here."

"Expect a call from Victor any minute now," Kim warned before hanging up.

As if on cue, Angela's phone rang a second later, and Victor's name flashed across the screen. Taking a deep breath, she picked up. "Victor, I just heard about the test results. I know you must be upset."

"Upset?" he snapped, anger lacing his words. "That's an understatement, Angela. I trusted you to figure this out, and now I'm left with a worthless forgery!"

"Listen, Victor," Angela said, her voice firm yet empathetic. "We're doing everything we can. In fact, I'm coming down to your shop right now to collect fingerprints myself. We'll get to the bottom of this."

Victor sighed with an air of defeat into the phone. "Fine. I'll meet you there."

"See you soon," Angela replied before hanging up. Turning to Ruff, she ruffled his fur. "Come on, boy. Duty calls."

As they drove toward Victor's shop, a sense of unease settled over Angela. The memory of the shadowy figure still niggled at her mind. Who was after her? Were they following her now?

"Stay sharp, Ruff," she whispered, her grip tightening on the steering wheel. As she stepped out of her car in front of the shop, Angela shivered at the slight chill in the air. She shook off the feeling and entered the shop, rolling her shoulders back.

"Angela," Victor said curtly. "Took you long enough."

"Victor, I'm here to help," she replied, gritting her teeth. "Let's just focus on sorting this mess out."

"Fine," he grumbled. "But when I told you my shop was robbed, you should've listened. Someone must've replaced the real thing with the forgery when they destroyed my shop."

"Victor, I'm sorry," Angela conceded. "I'll go over the security footage again, see if we can find out when the antiques were swapped and where the real one might've gone."

As they prepared to leave, Ruff growled, his gaze fixated on a raccoon perched near a window. Its beady eyes stared at something in the display, though he couldn't pinpoint what.

"Ruff, what's gotten into you?" Angela whispered. The raccoon scurried away, and he calmed down.

Angela and Victor made their way through the cluttered aisles of the antique shop. Victor slipped a copper key in the lock on the door to his office, where the epergne was now under lock and key.

As Angela began collecting fingerprints, Victor scowling at her from behind, arms crossed.

"You really think you'll find something?" he asked as she worked.

Angela paused, turning to face him. "Every contact leaves a trace, Victor. Even the most skilled thieves make mistakes."

Victor frowned. "I should have been more careful. I should have listened to the chief when he told me to install that security system sooner."

"It's not your fault," Angela interjected, clicking her tongue as she refocused on her task. "We'll sort this out. The real question is, who had access to the shop beside you?"

Victor stroked his chin. "Just a few trusted clients and my assistant. But I can't imagine any of them..."

Angela nodded. "Don't worry, we'll vet them. Has anything else been out of the ordinary lately?"

"Well, there was another inquiry about the epergne last week, but nothing came of it," Victor recalled, a frown creasing his forehead.

"Interesting," Angela murmured. "We'll look into that too. Every detail matters."

As she finished collecting the fingerprints, Victor exhaled. "I just hope this isn't for nothing,"

Angela offered him a reassuring smile. "Trust the process, Victor. We're doing our jobs. You just need to have a little patience."

"Patience has never been my strong suit," he conceded.

Angela smirked but didn't debate that point as she packed up her equipment and left the store.

Chapter 11

Angela entered the station about an hour later and navigated through the maze of desks, carrying a small envelope containing the fingerprint samples from Victor's shop. As she approached the front desk, she spotted Troy Jeffries, his face buried in the monumental stack of paperwork in front of him.

"Hey, Troy," Angela greeted, sliding the envelope across the desk. "Got something for forensics."

Troy looked up, grinning when recognition flashed across his face. "Angela, good timing. I'll get these down to the lab ASAP." He slipped the envelope into his pocket and Angela smiled.

"Thanks, Troy," she said, leaning against the desk as she peered at his monitor. "Any new leads on the Sterling case?"

Troy shook his head. "I wish. None of our leads have led anywhere. I still have a hunch about Conrad. He's too entangled in this to be just a coincidence."

"I was thinking the same," Angela replied. "But since the auction is over, I have no idea where to find him."

Troy's fingers flew over the keyboard as he pulled up the relevant files. "Looks like Conrad checked into the hotel where the auction was last Saturday." He swiveled the screen so Angela could see. "But there's no checkout date. He could still be there."

Angela's eyes narrowed. "Thanks, Troy. I think I'll head up there. See if I can shake him down."

With a quick wave goodbye, she hurried out of the station.

She drove back to the farm to grab Ruff's makeshift service dog vest in case they needed it at the hotel, and to check on the animals. Eggatha, her hen and the bossiest of all her animals around the farm, clucked contentedly as she pecked around the yard, closely followed by her chicks, Christi and Indy, the latter who was given her name thanks to her uncanny talent as a feathered escape artist. In their pen, her two black and white pigs rolled in the mud happily oinking as though they didn't have a care in the world, while the goats meandered nearby, occasionally nibbling on the fence.

As she was dumping the last of the slop in the pigs' trough, her phone vibrated in her pants pocket and she smiled as David's name lit up the caller ID.

"Hey, David," Angela answered, placing the slop bucket down and tossing some feed to the chickens. "What's up?"

"Oh nothing," he replied. "I'm on a break between classes, so I thought I'd check in. What are you up to?"

Angela sank down on the porch swing and crossed her legs. "you know. Same old same old; just taking care of the menagerie."

David laughed. "Sounds like fun," he said. "Any updates on the case?"

"I'm planning to visit Conrad at his hotel," Angela replied, watching Eggatha guide her chicks across the yard. Indy, as per usual, was much more interested in climbing the fence where her father, Angela's only rooster, perched. Angela laughed as her mother squawked at her in disapproval. "I think he might know more than he told us at the crime scene." She leaned into the back of the swing. "And the epergne that Victor bought at the auction? Someone replaced it with a fake."

David gasped. "You're kidding."

Angela shook her head. "We think it happened during the break-in the other night."

"Do you think that's why it looked like nothing was taken?" David asked.

"That's the theory. It's looking more like a planned heist than a random burglary," Angela said.

"Have you got anything on the thief?"

"Just that he has blue eyes," she mumbled with a shrug.

"Not much to go on," David agreed. The sound of a school bell chimed through the phone, and David sighed. "Gotta go. The last class is out. Be careful, Angela."

"I will," she replied. "Good luck with your day."

"Are we still on for dinner tomorrow?"

Angela smiled. "Absolutely."

They said their goodbyes and Angela hung up the phone. She then turned her attention to Ruff, who was lounging nearby, happily panting at the frolicking chickens.

"Ruff, come here, buddy. Time to get your vest on," Angela called out.

Ruff trotted over, but as soon as he saw the vest, his demeanor changed. He barked a defiant *woof* and danced out of Angela's reach. *Come on, not that thing again. Seriously, there can't be that many places in this town that don't allow dogs.*

"Oh, come on, Ruff. Don't make this hard," Angela chuckled, scrambling after him.

Ruff darted away and Angela feigned sternness. "Ruff, if you don't get this vest on, you're not coming with me to dinner tonight."

Ruff paused, tilting his head as his eyes widened. *No, she wouldn't, would she?*

He contemplated testing his theory for half a second, but ultimately decided that was not a risk he was willing to take. A low, reluctant grumble escaped his throat as he trotted toward her with his head hung low.

One of these days I'm going to get out of wearing this stupid thing.

"That's more like it," Angela said, scratching him between his ears as she slipped the vest over his head. "See, it's not so bad."

Ruff barked, his tail wagging half-heartedly at the prospect of seeing his grandparents and sneaking Abigail's food.

"Good boy. Now, let's get going. We have a big evening ahead of us."

Upon arriving at the hotel, Angela approached the reception desk, Ruff close at her heels.

"Hi, I'm Angela Atkinson. Can you please direct me to Conrad Cummings' room?"

The receptionist, a young woman with a practiced smile, began typing into her computer. After a moment, she looked up, "Room 312, on the third floor."

Angela smiled. "Thank you."

Turning, they headed toward the elevators. The hotel, usually bustling with guests and staff, seemed unusually quiet, and the hairs on the back of her neck stood on end. As they walked down the corridor, her steps echoed in the empty hallway.

For a minute, she thought she heard the distinctive clap of a second set of feet behind her. But each time she turned around, the hallway was empty, except for Ruff's soft panting.

As they approached room 312, Angela's hand instinctively went to the pepper spray in her pocket. The eerie feeling clung to her, and she paused outside the door, taking a deep breath to steady her nerves.

Her brow furrowed when she realized it was ajar and there was no 'Do Not Disturb' sign hung on the knob. Its hinges creaked as Angela gently pushed it open, her heart pounding in her ears as she stepped inside.

"Mr. Cummings? It's Angela Atkinson."

Silence. Ruff stayed close to Angela's side, his ears pricked as his gaze darted around the room.

She ventured inside. The sheets on the bed were disheveled as if someone had tried to make it but gotten distracted mid-task. A leather suitcase poked out from beneath the footboard and a frown creased her brow as she crouched down to examine it. Clothes were shoved haphazardly into the open bottom, but there was no ID, no wallet, and no money clip–

"He was definitely packing up," she murmured as Ruff scanned the perimeter of the room. "But it looks like something made him leave in a hurry."

Creak.

A floorboard giving way underfoot jolted Angela's attention to the far corner of the room. Every muscle in her body tensed. Ruff glared at the corner and a low, warning growl rumbled from his chest as his spine stiffened.

Angela held her breath as she edged toward the source of the sound, her hand gripping the pepper spray in her pocket as her heart thudded in her ears. Still, as she rounded the corner with her pepper spray at the ready, there was no one.

"Maybe it was just the water heater," Angela whispered to Ruff, trying to convince herself more than him. He barked, but didn't look entirely convinced.

Turning her focus back to the task at hand, Angela inched around the room, turning over every nook and cranny she could find. Ruff ducked under the dresser, then gave a sharp bark as he trotted over with a small red poker chip in his mouth. Angela grinned. "Nice find, boy." Her gambling dept theory had been nothing but speculation before, but this meant they were on the right track.

In the bedside drawer, hidden beneath a hastily thrown pile of clothes, Angela discovered a stash of cash. Her eyes widened as she pulled out the large green wad.

Enough to account for the missing epergne, perhaps?

She pocketed it for counting later, then turned when Ruff let out another sharp bark, before diving nose deep into the trash can!

"Ruff!" She ruled her eyes and hurried over, grabbing him by the scruff of his neck to pull him out of the mess of crumpled papers. "Well, what are you doing?" He turned to her, holding a crumpled piece of paper strewn with bold, blocky handwriting between his teeth.

Angela's brow furrowed as she pried it free, her stomach dropping while she skimmed the contents.

Conrad,

You're playing with fire. We know you messed up at Victor's. Time's running out. Pay up by the end of the week or you'll regret it. This is your final warning.

Don't disappoint us again.

It was dated a day after the theft at Victor's.

She looked down at Ruff, a shiver rippling down her spine as the pieces slowly fell into place. Conrad was on the run from loan sharks. He must have stolen the epergne from Victor's shop and then pawned it off before skipping town. Except... why leave so much extra money behind?

Angela pulled out her phone and dialed Chief Helbar. She paced the room as it rang, her gaze drifting over the disordered contents of Conrad's hotel room.

"Hello?" he barked after a third ring.

"Chief? It's Angela. I've got a solid lead on Victor's shop case. I think Conrad, Sterling's business partner, is involved. He's got gambling debts, and when I came to check on him at his hotel, it looked like he skipped home. There was a threatening note in his trash."

She relayed her theory, explaining how she believed Conrad stole the epergne to pay off his debts before fleeing.

When she was done, the line was dead silent.

"Chief?"

"It's an excellent find, Angela," he intoned. "I just wish it didn't leave the trail of the murder case so cold."

Angela cringed as she ran a hand through her hair. "Sorry."

"Don't be. A lead in one case is better than nothing. I'll put out an APB for him right away."

Chapter 12

That night, the sun had dipped below the horizon by the time Angela pulled up to her parents' house. Ruff leaped out of the car, tail wagging madly against her leg as he bounded toward the door. Angela sighed, breathing in the familiar scent of home as she entered the house. For a moment, she allowed herself to forget the troubles of her investigation and simply enjoy the company of her family.

"Angela, darling!" her mother Abigail exclaimed, enveloping her in a tight hug as they entered the cozy kitchen. "I've made a cinnamon rum bundt cake for dessert. It's a new recipe I'm trying for Christmas."

"Smells amazing, Mom," Angela replied, her mouthwatering at the thought. "Where's Dad?"

"Your father is in the living room," Abigail said, ushering her daughter toward the doorway. Angela found her father, Charlie, sitting in his favorite armchair, a newspaper spread across his lap. He looked up as she entered, his eyes crinkling with warmth.

"Angie," he said with a grin. "How's the case going?"

"Slowly, Dad," Angela admitted, sinking into the couch. "Everywhere I look is a dead end, and honestly?" She cast a hopeful glance toward her father. "I could use some help."

Charlie grinned, rubbing his brow. "Of course. Anything I can do."

Abigail bustled back into the living room, carrying plates laden with steaming food. After they ate, she brought out the dessert, which she presented with a flourish.

"Mom, this cake is amazing," Angela complimented between bites after dinner, savoring the rich flavors of cinnamon and rum as they danced on her tongue.

"Thank you, dear," her mother beamed. "Now, what was it you needed help with?"

"Dad's old case files," Angela replied, looking at her dad as she swallowed a bite of cake. "I haven't looked at them yet, but I need to know everything about that lead you were chasing before you retired."

Charlie leaned back in his chair, his expression turning somber. "Alright, Angie. But I must be honest. It's not much."

"Please Dad," she begged. "Anything you know could help."

"We were trying to pin down a guy named James. At least, that was his alias at the time. We suspected he was one of the higher-ups in the forgery ring, but couldn't quite pin down how high up he was. What we did know was that he wanted out of the game."

"Go on," Angela urged, leaning forward as her pulse picked up speed. "How did you know he wanted out?"

Charlie sighed, rubbing his forehead. "We'd been tracking him long enough to learn he had a long-term girlfriend. She was pregnant, and we suspected that made him want to go straight."

Angela hummed.

"James was holding back information, afraid of being targeted by the forgery ring," Charlie continued. "We just about convinced him to meet with us, guaranteeing witness protection. But a few days later, he was targeted by a sniper, right at his own home."

Angela's eyes widened. "Was it someone from the forgery ring?"

"Can't say for sure," her father admitted. He had a haunted look in his eyes that Angela was not fond of. "But it happened when he was with his girl. The whole thing spooked him, and he went on the run after that. No one's heard from him since."

"Darn it," Angela muttered under her breath. So close, yet so far. She shuffled through the papers strewn across the table. One of them caught her eye, and she pulled it free from the pile. Penelope Bedingfield. That was the name she had scrawled in her office.

"Dad," she said urgently, "have you ever heard this name before?"

"Penelope Bedingfield...?" Charlie repeated, his face paling. "That's James' girlfriend!"

"Really?" Angela gasped, her gaze darting between her father's face and the paper. "Are her last known whereabouts in your old file?"

"I think so."

Angela's heart raced. Maybe they could find Penelope and James. If her father was right and he really was trying to go straight, maybe he would give them the breakthrough they so desperately needed.

Her eyes welled as she rose from the table and hugged her father around his shoulders, his wiry frame leaning into hers for support. "Thank you, Dad," she whispered. "I never would've found this without you."

"Of course, sweetheart," Charlie replied, hugging her back. "Anything for you."

"Mom, let me help clean up," Angela offered, glancing over at her mother, who was carefully collecting the plates scattered about the table.

"Thank you, dear," Abigail replied. "I'm glad your father could help you with that case." As they cleared the remnants of their meal, Angela couldn't help but notice the occasional tremble in her mother's hands, a stark reminder of the early onset of dementia. She bit her lip and made eye contact with her father. Was it getting worse? He gave her a subtle shake of his head over her mother's shoulder and Angela breathed a sigh of relief. She knew if they were lucky, it could be a slow-progressing disease. But every symptom still sent her blood pressure spiking.

"Tomorrow, I'm going to visit Penelope," Angela said as they dried the dishes. "Maybe she can give us some answers."

"Can I come with you?" Charlie asked. "I'd love to have a hand in taking these scoundrels down."

Angela hesitated as her gaze lingered on her mother, who seemed momentarily lost, staring blankly at the cinnamon rum bundt cake crumbs on the table. Her father followed her gaze and smiled sadly as he squeezed her shoulder. "I'll find someone to be with her while we're gone."

"Alright, Dad," Angela agreed. It would be nice to have some backup, and she hadn't gone out in the field with her father for far too long. They continued cleaning in companionable silence.

As Angela and Ruff prepared to leave, the anticipation of confronting Penelope set Angela's nerves on edge, but she also couldn't wait for the case to be over.

Chapter 13

The scent of oil paint and aged canvas permeated the air as Angela stepped into the cluttered studio, Ruff by her side. "Hi," she called out, glancing around the studio but unsure exactly who she was looking for. Several patrons milled about the room, but a young woman turned to face them, her auburn hair falling haphazardly in front of her freckled face. Petite in stature and with a lithe frame, Angela highly doubted such a young woman had anything to do with such a high-powered organization. But if she learned anything in her time as a private investigator, it was to never underestimate someone.

"Oh, hi officers. I'm Penelope, but everybody calls me Penny. What can I do for you?"

"Hi Penny," she walked up to her and held out a hand, which the young woman gently took. "I'm Angela, and this is my father, Charlie Atkinson. We're just here to ask you a few questions."

Penny climbed off the stool she was sitting on in front of her easel and beckoned them to follow her to the back. "Of course, glad to be of help."

Once they were inside her smaller and much more cramped office, which looked more like a kindergartner's art studio than anywhere professional, Penny gestured for them to take a seat on the covered modern-style chairs across from her desk. "Please have a seat. What can I do for you?"

Angela looked at her father, thinking it was only right that he had the first chance to question Penelope, since this was originally his case. Charlie smiled softly and then leaned forward, crossing his hands on the desk. "Look, Miss Bedingfield, I understand that this might be a bit of a shock, but do you know anything recent about a man named Sterling Hastings?"

Penny's eyes bulged and her cheeks lost some of their color. She shifted in her seat and gulped. "No, not recently. Why do you ask?"

He gestured to Angela, who cleared her throat. "Listen, Miss, we know this might be a lot to take in, but he died about three days ago. We know you used to have a connection to him and so we wondered…"

Penelope's mouth dropped open. "Wait, you guys think I had something to do with this?" Angela and her father said nothing, but the screech of Penelope's stool against the concrete of the floor told them more than words ever could. "No, you've got this all wrong." Penelope's voice cracked under the weight of her nerves. "I… I'm just an artist."

"An artist who creates counterfeit antiques," Charlie interjected, staring her down with a fiercer look than Angela had ever seen before.

Penny wrung her hands together. "Look, I know nothing about Sterling's death. People ask me to create things, and I do it. It's just business."

"Business that resulted in a man's death," Angela said. She could see the fear in Penny's eyes, but it wasn't enough. They needed a solid confession.

Penny shook her head again. "Listen, I didn't know what they were going to use those pieces for. I swear, I-I never wanted anyone to get hurt," she stammered, and tears sprang to the edges of her eyes

Angela studied the young woman, trying to decipher if she truly was ignorant of the implications of her work or if she was simply a skilled liar.

She scanned the cramped studio; brushes with bristles stained in a kaleidoscope of colors lay haphazardly on a paint-splattered table, while jars of pigments and aging agents lined overcrowded shelves.

"Quite a collection you've got here," she remarked, her gaze lingering on a half-finished forgery that sat amidst the chaos. The details were exquisite, and if she didn't know what she was looking for, she scarcely would have noticed the difference.

"Thanks," Penny muttered, her gaze still averted as she fiddled with the hem of her blouse.

"Your skills are remarkable," Angela continued, her fingers tracing the edge of a nearby painting that looked to be a replica of a van Gogh. "I would think there would be many uses for someone with a talent as clever as yours."

For a moment, Penny remained silent, her face a whirlwind of conflicting emotions. After what seemed like an eternity, she exhaled a shaky breath and met Angela's eyes.

"I never meant for it to go this far. I was just trying to make a living. And I swear to you, no matter what I have or haven't done, I did not kill Sterling."

"Sometimes, it's not about what we intend," Angela said softly, "It's about what we do when we realize our actions have consequences, and how we choose to handle them."

As Angela spoke, Ruff whined softly at her feet, his dark eyes fixed on Penny. She may have been guilty of something, but whatever it was, he was pretty sure it wasn't murder.

"Whether you were a willing participant or an unwitting pawn," Angela went on, "there's no denying that your work has played a role in this. And if we're going to get to the bottom of it, we need your help."

Penny hesitated, her fingers twisting together. Ruff gently nudged her leg, and Angela saw her soften as she looked into his big brown eyes. With a resigned sigh, she nodded, her expression determined as she squared her shoulders.

"Alright," she agreed, her voice stronger now. "I'll help you. But I want you to know that I never wanted anyone to get hurt because of my work."

Angela studied Penny's face, searching for any hint of malice, but she was only met with fear. She reached across the table and gently took the younger girl's fingers in her own. They were clammy and cold, but she didn't pull away.

"I know you're scared, but we need your help."

Penny swallowed hard, her fingers fidgeting with the hem of her blouse again. "There's... there's someone," she whispered, her voice quivering. "A buyer who commissioned several pieces from me. I never met them in person, but they always paid well and kept their distance."

Angela's thoughts raced, and she exchanged significant looks with her father. "Can you remember any details about them?"

"Only that they went by a codename. The Connoisseur," Penny admitted, her eyes downcast. "I know nothing else. I swear."

"Alright," Angela said, nodding slowly. "We'll work with that. Thank you, Penny."

As they got ready to leave, Ruff blocked the door, staring intently at something outside the studio. His ears were perked, and his tail remained perfectly still.

"Ruff," Angela called softly, winding her leash around her hand. "What do you see?"

It's not what I see. It's what I smell. Ruff gave a low growl, his gaze never leaving the door. Whoever had been near them the other night was here now, he was sure of it. With a flick of his tail, he inched toward the door.

Stay behind me.

As Angela stepped out of Penny's studio into the crisp autumn air, she couldn't shake the feeling that they were being watched. The hair on the back of her neck stood up, goosebumps rose on her arms, and she felt like no matter where she turned, someone's eyes were on her. Her suspicions were confirmed when she spotted the same man who had been lurking outside her office earlier. The figure stood half in shadow, trying unsuccessfully to blend with the surroundings.

"Hey, Dad," Angela murmured, nudging Charlie as they walked away toward her car. "I think we're being followed."

Charlie raised an eyebrow and subtly glanced over his shoulder. "You mean the fellow in the black biker jacket?"

"Yep." Apprehension flickered through Angela's chest, but she forced herself to maintain her composure. "Let Ruff off his leash. He can track him without drawing attention."

Charlie nodded and unclipped Ruff's leash, allowing the border collie to take the lead. With surprising stealth for a dog his size, Ruff darted through the shadows, eyes locked on the stranger. Angela and Charlie trailed behind, keeping a safe distance while still maintaining sight of their canine companion.

"Who do you think he is?" Charlie asked, his voice barely above a whisper.

"I don't know," Angela admitted, her mind racing through possible connections between the man and the counterfeit antiques. "But he must have something to do with all this."

The narrow streets of Hummings Hollow twisted and turned, becoming like a maze as they crossed them, almost faster than she could process. As Ruff led them further away from the town center, Angela looked behind her, relieved when she found her father was keeping pace.

"Stay close, Dad," Angela warned, her protective instincts flaring as they navigated the alleys. "And be prepared for anything."

"Always am," Charlie replied, the corner of his mouth turning upward.

A few blocks later, Ruff halted suddenly, his ears perked and tail rigid. Angela and Charlie exchanged glances before cautiously approaching the dimly lit alley where Ruff had stopped. Shadows danced on the cobblestone as the flickering light from a nearby lamppost struggled to penetrate the darkness.

"Who's there?" Angela called out, her voice steady despite the sound of her heart beating in her ears. She gripped her father's arm as they peered into the murky depths of the alley.

"Didn't expect to see you here, Angela," a familiar voice replied. Stepping out from the shadows, a tall, wiry man emerged, and Angela held back a gasp. She knew that face. Angela and her father had helped the police track down an elusive art thief a few months ago as part of the forgery ring crackdown, and had almost cornered him before he got away and skipped town. She had no idea he was back, let alone this close to her.

"Michael," Angela said, narrowing her eyes. "What are you doing in town?"

"Business, my dear." He flashed a wolfish grin. "And you two are getting in my way."

"Cut the act, Michael," Angela's father demanded. "We've been following you since you left Penny's studio. What's your connection to all this? The forgeries, Sterling's murder?"

"Murder?" Michael echoed with a scoff. He clicked his tongue and shook his head. "I have no part in such grisly affairs. I'm just here for the real epergne."

Angelo looked him up and down, her pulse slowing slightly now that she had identified her intruder. "Why don't I believe you?"

"You don't have to," he said with a laugh. "You've seen my police record. I may be a lot of things, but I've never touched a murder weapon."

Angela gnashed her teeth, half tempted to wipe that smug smirk right off his face.

"Who are you working for, Michael?" she growled. "And better yet, how did you get back in Hummings Hollow without the chief knowing?"

"Ah, now that's the million-dollar question, isn't it?" Michael replied, his smile fading as quickly as it had appeared. "Unfortunately, I'm not at liberty to say."

"Whatever you're planning, we'll stop you," Charlie chimed in, his hand resting firmly on Ruff's back.

"Good luck with that," Michael smirked.

"Let's take him to Chief Helbar," Angela suggested, keeping her gaze locked on Michael. "Maybe he can loosen those lips."

In a flash, Michael's eyes darted from Angela to Charlie and then to the exit of the alley. They both started forward, but he made a break for it and was half the second quicker than them, bolting for it as if a hellhound itself was on his heels.

"Ruff, after him!" Angela shouted as she struggled to keep up.

The border collie eagerly leaped into action, nipping at Michael's heels as they raced through the narrow passages between buildings. Angela and Charlie followed closely behind, their breaths coming in ragged gasps. The chase weaved through alleyways and over fences, the distance between them closing and widening in turns. "Can't let him get away again," she mumbled, gritting her teeth as she vaulted over a low wall.

"Stay on him, Ruff!" Charlie encouraged. His voice was strained, but a steely determination flashed in his eyes.

"Where did he go?" Angela panted, pausing to get her breath. She braced her hands on her knees as they careened into the open square, only for Michael to have vanished completely. She scanned the area, searching desperately for any sign of him and finding none.

"Over there!" Charlie pointed, his eyes narrowing as a figure disappeared around yet another corner. They resumed the chase, their lungs burning and legs aching.

Almost got him, Angela thought, and they rounded another bend. *Just a little further.*

But a few blocks later, he disappeared again. Ruff, Angela, and Charlie stood panting in a dimly lit street, their heaving breaths filling the air.

Angela cursed under her breath, frustration coursing through her. "We were so close."

"Angela, we'll find him," Charlie reassured her, placing a hand on her shoulder. "He can't hide forever."

Angela frowned as she gazed toward the last corner Michael had turned. Her father was right, but he could stay underground long enough to evade any evidence tying him to the case. He had done it before. What was stopping him from doing it again?

As they regrouped, she caught a glint of something on the cobblestones near the corner where he had disappeared. Bending down, she picked up a crumpled piece of paper and unfolded it. Her eyes grew wide when she took in the elegant details of the drawing.

"Look at this," she breathed, beckoning her father over.

"What is it? Did he leave something behind?"

Angela shook her head. "Nothing that will help us catch him." She tilted the paper toward her father, and he rubbed his hand along his chin. "But it might help us find what he was after." A smile curled up the corners of her lips as she pointed at the name scribbled at the top of the blueprint. "It's the epergne. And if I'm right, it's a full-scale model."

Charlie's eyes widened as he examined the paper. "This is good, Angela. If he has a model of the real thing, maybe he knows where it is."

Her smile dipped down into a frown just as quickly as it had appeared. "Yeah, maybe, but first we have to find him."

Charlie leaned over and gave her a hug. "Don't worry, we will."

Angela leaned into her father's touch, then straightened up and rolled her shoulders back as she folded the blueprint and tucked it in the back pocket of her pants.

"Let's get back to the office," she suggested. "We can plan better there. Create a real strategy. If we're going to catch this guy, we're going to need a plan."

Her father nodded. "Spoken like a true detective."

Back at her office, Angela pinned the sketch to a corkboard alongside other pieces of evidence. "Everything seems to lead back to Victor's shop. I mean, I know he didn't murder Sterling because I was with him the whole time. But everything to do with the epergne just keeps pointing right back there." Angela stalled her pacing and studied the board one more time. "He's not going to like it," she muttered, with a bemused smile, "but I think we need to visit him again."

"Sounds like a plan," Charlie agreed, grabbing his coat. "I'll call Chief Helbar and let him know what we've found so far. He might be able to help."

"Good idea, Dad. Let's meet there in an hour," Angela said, grabbing her own coat and giving Ruff a reassured pat.

"Be careful, Angela," Charlie called after her, as they went their separate ways to their cars. "I'm just going to dart home and check on your mother." William had agreed to hang out with Abigail for the day, but Charlie still wanted to make sure that they weren't driving each other crazy.

"Always am, Dad," she replied, offering a small smile before stepping out. "I'm gonna go home and take care of the animals. Nothing too exciting, I promise."

Chapter 14

A cool breeze rustled Angela's blonde hair as her gaze roamed over the interior of the shop. It no longer bore any signs of the break-in a few days prior.

"Looks like they've cleaned up quickly," she mused, scratching Ruff's head. The dog wagged his tail in agreement, his keen eyes never leaving the shop's window.

The bell above the door jingled merrily as they stepped inside, but Victor greeted them with a scowl when his gaze lifted from his latest book. "Oh no. Now what do you want? Unless you found out some fresh development about my epergne, I don't want to hear it."

Ruff huffed, and Angela bit back the retort dancing on the edge of her tongue. "Actually, we were wondering if we could take another look at it."

Victor rolled his eyes but shrugged his shoulders and let out an exaggerated sigh as he beckoned them behind the desk. "If you must." He led them to the display where the epergne stood proudly in a new case in his back office. Angela studied it carefully, comparing the subtle differences she could now spot from the sketch Michael had dropped. Had she not been looking for the imperfections, she would have dismissed it as genuine.

"Remarkable work," she muttered, tracing a finger over the delicate curves of the silver epergne. *Penny is truly talented. I can see why the forgery ring scouted her out.*

For as sure as she was that the girl wasn't directly involved, Angela couldn't shake the feeling that there was more to her story; she just had to find the proof.

"Indeed," Victor sighed. "whoever made this is wasting their talents on illegal activity."

Ruff suddenly gave a low growl, his attention drawn to the same raccoon by the window. Angela raised an eyebrow.

"Odd," she murmured. "That raccoon seems to have taken a liking to that teapot."

"Animals have a strange sense for things," Victor mused, glaring at the animal over the rims of his glasses. "It would be a lot easier if it would be fascinated with something other than my trash cans at night."

Angela's investigative instincts flared. "Victor, would you mind if I looked at that teapot?" she asked.

"By all means," he replied. "I've had it in my storage room for years. I never noticed anything particularly special about it, but that raccoon sure does."

As Angela approached the teapot, she couldn't help but think of her father. He had taught her the importance of noticing the smallest details and trusting her instincts. It was a lesson she carried with her throughout her career as a private investigator.

"Let's see what you're hiding," she whispered, watching Victor unlock the window to the display so she could reach inside.

As Angela gingerly lifted it from its pedestal, her fingers brushed against its curves. It felt heavier than she had anticipated, and Ruff whined softly, his gaze never leaving the porcelain.

"Is everything all right?" Victor asked

"Something's off," she murmured, turning the teapot over in her hands. She held her breath and traced her fingers over every inch and bump several times. Finally, she discovered a tiny, almost imperceptible seam that wasn't meant to be there, just within the interior of the lid.

"Victor, look at this," she said, tilting it so he could see. "There's a secret compartment."

"Remarkable," Victor marveled. "To think I've had it all this time, and I never noticed it."

"My father always said to trust my instincts," Angela said, a nostalgic smile tugging at her lips. "That advice has never failed me."

"I should hope not," her father said, smiled as he lingered in the shop's doorway. "Now, what have we here?"

Angela smiled and beckoned her father inside. "Dad, come in! We're investigating something hidden inside this teapot. There's a raccoon outside who seems oddly intrigued by it. We're trying to figure out why." She paused. "How are Mom and William? Is everything okay?"

Her father smiled. "They're doing fine. William's been talking about taking you out in his Challenger. You know how much he loves that car and hardly lets anyone else drive it."

As her father stepped further into the room, they turned their attention back to the teapot.

Finally, with Victor's skilled hands, they managed to open the compartment. Angela peered inside and carefully extracted a small, aged piece of parchment. Ruff perked up, eyes fixed on the delicate paper. Angela gently unfolded it, revealing a letter addressed to someone named Anna.

"Look at this," she whispered. It was a letter from the original owner of the teapot to a woman who appeared to be her granddaughter.

Dearest Anna,

I entrust to you our family's legacy hidden within this teapot. 29,78,45,32,67,50. Keep these numbers close to your heart and remember that no matter what, love transcends everything.

Forever yours,

Grandmother

There was an address scribbled on the back of the parchment, but Angela couldn't make it out. A ping of sentimentality washed over her as she imagined what kind of bond this woman must've had with her granddaughter. She couldn't help but compare it to the relationship she had with her own parents.

"What is it?" Victor asked.

Her father stepped in closer as she handed over the parchment, a smug smile playing on her lips as his eyes widened in surprise.

"Oh my word... To think I've had this all this time and I've never seen it before." Victor looked up at Angela, his face suddenly serious and tinged with a hint of nostalgia she had doubted ever having seen before. "We must return this teapot to its rightful owner."

"Agreed," Angela said with a smile. "But while you do that, I'm gonna continue to work on the Sterling case."

She had planned to meet the chief at the auction house in about twenty minutes, and she didn't want to be late.

Victor pressed his lips together and gave her a stiff nod. "Will do. I'll keep you posted if I find anything interesting." Angela smiled as they turned to leave. "Thank you so much, Victor." Perhaps he wasn't as curmudgeonly as everyone made him out to be after all.

***

Exactly nineteen minutes and forty-five seconds later, Angela pulled up in front of the now-familiar auction house.

Chief Helbar's cruiser was already parked outside the entrance, and he was standing near the reception desk with a resolute look on his face as she breezed through the door.

"Let's start with Sterling's office," the chief suggested gruffly, marching to the back of the building as if he owned the place

"Good idea," Angela replied, as she followed a few paces behind. Ruff trotted right beside her, his ears perked and alert. Angela flicked on the light and they glanced around. She felt like she had already canvased every surface, but she knew even the most astute detective could miss things when they didn't know what they were looking for.

Angela started at the filing cabinet while the chief took the desk. She went through every drawer, but most of the records looked just the same as what Kim had found online. Only when she reached one at the far end of the last row did her curiosity pique.

"Chief, come over here."

Angela yanked the drawer as the chief approached, wiping a sheen of sweat off her brow. "I can't get this open; it seems stuck."

It took all their combined strength to pry the door open, and when they did, Angela peered inside with a frown. "It's empty."

The chief leaned in next to her, a small smile gracing his lips when he shook his head. "Not quite."

He reached down and pressed a small gold button wedge between the front of the drawer and the floor. Angela gasped. She hadn't even seen it, but when it disappeared from the bottom of the drawer with a satisfying click, the floor gave way to a false ceiling. Within the hidden drawer were a myriad of overstuffed folders and documents.

"Oh, my goodness. How many hidden compartments are there?"

The chief flashed Angela a satisfied smirk and folded his arms. "See, sometimes an old dog can learn new tricks." Angela smiled as she reached down into the newfound storage space and began sifting through the folders, one by one. The deeper she went, the more amazed she was by the result.

Each of them were meticulously maintained records of transactions that either Sterling or Conrad had taken part in—transactions that Angela suspected were never meant to see the light of day.

"Chief, look," Angela exclaimed, sliding a damning piece of evidence toward him. "This is the account Sterling's been sending payments to." She traced her finger along a line in the bank records. "It's a company called Silent Shipments."

The chief let out a rueful laugh as his eyes narrowed. "That's definitely a little too convenient for my taste."

"Exactly," Angela said. "We should look into them."

The chief agreed, and they continued searching the office. One thing hidden was a lucky find, but two were a coincidence. And if Angela knew anything about police work, it was that there were no such things as coincidences. She doubted these two compartments were the only hidden things in his office, and now she was determined to uncover all she could. Her gaze fell upon a dusty bookshelf lined with leather-bound volumes, their spines cracked and worn.

She wandered over, examining each row. As she ran her fingers over every volume, Ruff paddled to her side and nudged the small bronze bird protruding out from the end of the bookshelf.

It sank inward and Angela jumped back as a section of the shelf swung open, revealing a hidden compartment housing a slim, unassuming ledger. With a triumphant grin, Angela pulled it from its hiding place and leafed through the pages, Ruff watching her intently from the floor, his chest puffed out with pride.

See, I knew you would need me on this case.

Each entry detailed transactions that had never been publicly recorded—payments for specific items, many of which matched the descriptions of the allegedly forged items, and antiques that the house documents had not accounted for. As Angela continued reading, her pulse quickened. If this were anything to go by, the scope of the smuggling operation was far more extensive than she'd initially thought; if only the ledger would've been kind enough to mention the names of the people involved as well. Nonetheless, she pocketed the ledger for evidence after showing it to the chief.

"Whoever's behind this," he mused as they made their way back out into the daylight, "must have had a good reason to kill Sterling."

Angela nodded. "Yeah, if what Conrad said was true, and this was his last auction before he... retired..." A sudden shiver raced down her spine. "If the leaders knew he went out of the game, then maybe—?"

"Maybe they put out a hit for his head?" the chief suggested. Angela pressed her lips together and nodded.

Chief Helber ran two fingers over his mustache. "It is certainly a possibility. If he became the whistleblower, then he could blow the entire operation. That's why we were tracking down that James guy a few years back."

Angela nodded again. Her father had said the same thing.

"The only question is, who was the hitman?"

A theory started forming in Angela's mind, but she shook it away. It was too obvious, too contrived. But then again, that might have made it the perfect cover.

Chapter 15

After a few more minutes of searching but finding nothing of consequence, Angela and the chief decided that they had done all that they could at the auction house. Chief Helbar took out his evidence kit, and they packed up the leather-bound book along with all the other incriminating documents they had found to take back to the lab for further inspection.

As they headed out to the parking lot, Angela quickly explained her theory—that perhaps Conrad had poisoned Sterling at the behest of the forgery ring leader to pay off his own debt, and he framed himself to appear as an innocent bystander to avoid further detection.

"You might be onto something, Angela," Chief Helbar admitted as they drew closer to his cruiser. "Your theory has legs." He paused as he rubbed his chin and leaned against the side of the police car. "There's just one problem. If he was so determined to look innocent, why go on the run a few days into the investigation?"

Angela shrugged. "He saw us at the crime scene, didn't he? Must've realized we'd start digging. A guilty conscience can make a man do crazy things."

The chief nodded, but his gaze narrowed. "I'll get in touch with the feds and see if we can track Conrad's movements. He can't have vanished into thin air."

Angela hummed. "In the meantime, I'll delve deeper into Sterling and Conrad's associates. Someone must know where they were before the auction."

Chief Helbar's expression hardened as he yanked open the cruiser door. "Conrad said something about them drinking whiskey, didn't he?"

Angela nodded. "Yes, and Sterling was found with strychnine in his system, which is pretty easy to hide in a liquor that strong."

Chief Helbar nodded slowly. "If you don't find anything in Sterling's room, maybe check the bars. Perhaps Conrad paid one bartender to slip something into his drink."

Angela mulled the thought over in her mind. "I'll keep that in mind, Chief. Thanks."

With that, she headed back to the hotel, Ruff loyally trotting at her side.

The receptionist directed her to the penthouse suite. She took the elevator to the top floor and followed the directions until she reached a set of double doors. She exchanged a look with Ruff before trying one of the handles, surprised to find it open despite the fact that the receptionist assured her no one had checked in yet. It was eerie to see such an extravagant room so deserted.

"Looks like someone left in a hurry," Angela mumbled to Ruff, gesturing to the neatly folded sheets on the bed and the untouched plates of food on the dining table.

Ruff sniffed around and wagged his tail, and Angela followed closely behind. But there was nothing out of the ordinary - just a few crumbs from some pastries in one pocket of an old coat draped over a chair. She turned her attention to the rest of the room, checking drawers and closets, but all she found were more belongings - clothes, shoes, toiletries. Nothing that seemed significant or out of place.

Then, Angela's eyes landed on the decanter on the bar. She pulled up the photograph from the crime scene on her phone, glad she had been smart enough to take a picture of the other decanter in it before the chief had taken it down to evidence. Angela's eyes darted back and forth between the two objects. Each bore the same intricate pattern of vines and leaves etched into the glass, and both of the stoppers were the same blooming peony; they were nearly identical. The decanter in the photograph was the same one Sterling had refused to sell on the day of the auction.

Ruff wedged in beside her and stuck his nose over the rim of the glass. He sniffed at it and recoiled, shaking his head and stifling a sneeze as a pungent and definitely unfamiliar scent lingered in his nostrils.

Eww! What is that?

Angela's brow furrowed. "What is it, boy?"

Ruff barked as he glared at the decanter. *You don't smell that?* He backed up even further despite the offending container now being nowhere near his nose. *Ugh. It's putrid.*

The decanter appeared empty, but Angela picked it up and sniffed. The scent of stale whiskey was as strong as ever, but it didn't appear to have any other odors. Still, she swabbed the rim of the decanter before pulling out her phone and calling the chief.

"Chief, I have a hunch. We're at Sterling's apartment, and Ruff can't seem to stand the smell of the decanter I found in his bar. Isn't strychnine supposed to be odorless?"

Chief Helbar hummed. "To humans, yes. But to dogs? I'm not sure. Take a swab of the inside of the decanter and we'll get it down to evidence."

Angela nodded and slipped the sample she had taken into an evidence bag. "Already on it."

"Good."

Angela leaned against the counter. "Something bothers me," she mused. "If Conrad and Sterling both drank from the decanter, how come he didn't feel the effects of the poison as well?"

The chief's voice crackled through the phone. "That's a good question. Keep heading down that trail. Let me know what else you find."

"Will do, Chief," she hung up the phone and spun around to scan the rest of the suite. "Alright Ruff, let's see what else he left for us."

Angela and Ruff continued milling through Sterling's belongings but found nothing worth noting until she dug in the back of a closet. There, she found a drawer covered with a thin layer of dust and cobwebs.

Hmm. Angela knelt down, slid it open, and revealed a small, unassuming-looking laptop. Angela gently lifted it from its hiding place. She wiped the top clean, opened it, and when it flickered to life, a password-protected screen glared back at her.

"I should've known," Angela muttered as she glanced around. Her gaze landed on a stack of classic art books on the nearby nightstand. She inched over toward them and flipped to the title pages, noticing most of the books were on Van Gogh. Holding her breath, she moved back toward the laptop and hovered her fingers over the keyboard. *There's no way it could be that simple,* she thought. But as she tapped the letters out on the keyboard and hit enter, the screen flickered to life. Angela's pulse picked up speed as she navigated to his email box and wasted no time scrolling through it. Most of the messages were mundane, comprising auction schedules and invoices, but there was one email thread from an unknown sender. The subject line read: "Special Delivery." Angela clicked on it as her heart pounded in her ears.

Subject: Re: Special Delivery

S,

The epergne has arrived. I brought in an expert to confirm it's the real deal. Now all we need to do is recruit a forger. I know you've said Penny has been showing real talent lately. I trust you can handle recruiting her for our little project?

Also, keep an eye out for anyone who may be on your tail. The boss said we might have a mole in our operation. We don't want anyone getting wind of our plans.

G.S.

Angela sat back on her heels and went through the rest of the thread. It looked like whoever this GS person was, they were the ones who were helping Conrad get access to the real epergne, which he had intended to make a forgery of to sell at the auction. Now she just had to find out where this email originated from.

And she knew just the person for the job. Pulling out her phone, she navigated to her favorites and hit Michelle's number, who answered halfway through the second ring.

"Michelle, hey, it's Angela."

"Oh, hey Ang. What's up? Any new leads on the case?"

Angela sat back and glanced at the list of emails staring at her from the screen. "Maybe, but I need your help. I found Sterling's laptop and there's a string of cryptic emails buried in his inbox. Can you track down the web address and see who they're from?"

"Of course," Michelle replied. "Bring the laptop here. I'll call Bobby and see if he can work his magic."

Angela managed a smile. Bobby was a young college student who used to have a crush on her but was now dating Kathy, her ex-coworker from The Lake House. He also happened to be quite the tech genius.

"Sounds good. Let me know when he can meet, and I'll bring the laptop to your office."

"I'll keep you posted." They hung up, and Angela tucked the laptop under her arm instead of putting it back in the dusty drawer.

"Alright, Ruff. We finally have a lead. Ready to track it down?"

Always.

Chapter 16

T he morning air was brisk as Ruff and Angela made their way to Michelle's office at the Hummings Hollow Gazette. The Gazette, nestled in the heart of the town, always had a buzz of activity around it, but today it seemed especially busy.

Upon arriving, Angela nudged the main door open and navigated to the door boasting the editor-in-chief placard. The office was a clutter of papers, coffee mugs, and the faint hum of a computer. Michelle was sitting behind the desk in the center of the room, surrounded by a flurry of documents. When Ruff barked softly, she looked up and offered a quick nod. "Hey, guys. Right on time. Bobby should be here any minute."

Angela set the laptop on a cluttered desk, its screen reflecting the overhead lights. She glanced around just as Bobby came in, his eyes flickering as they landed on Ruff.

"Hey, Bobby, thanks for coming. Do you think you can help us trace this IP address?" Angela asked.

"Sure thing, Angela." Bobby ambled over, his gait awkward yet eager as he dropped onto the couch.

Ruff trotted up to Bobby, his tail swishing the air behind him. Bobby couldn't help but smile as he reached out to scratch behind Ruff's ears. "Hey there, buddy," he mumbled as Ruff leaned into the impromptu massage.

As Angela opened the laptop, Ruff nudged Bobby's hand with his nose. Bobby laughed, giving Ruff a final pet before turning his attention to the screen. His fingers flew across the keyboard with practiced ease, the clicking sounds filling the small office.

"The emails... they're from Geoffrey Thorne, an art collector," Bobby announced after a few minutes. He turned to Angela and swiveled the screen so she could see. "He's a bit of a mystery, but his name's popped up here and there. Ring any bells?"

Michelle approached, leaning over to get a better look at the screen. "Geoffrey Thorne? He's quite the enigma. Collects art and, apparently, secrets, too."

Angela mulled it over. "Good to know. I'll definitely look into it. Thanks."

"Anytime, Angela. Good luck."

Michelle walked Bobby out and Angela dialed Chief Helbar. "Chief, it's Angela. I found Sterling's laptop and a thread of emails. We were able to trace the IP address back to an art collector named Geoffrey Thorne."

"Interesting," Chief Helbar replied. "What do we know about him?"

"Michelle and Bobby didn't find much information on him, but it's a start. I think we should pay him a visit."

"Agreed. Let's meet up in half an hour. That'll give me enough time to track down the address, and then we can head over there together."

"Sounds good. See you soon." Angela hung up and glanced down at Ruff, who was now watching her with curious eyes.

Half an hour later, Angela pulled up to the address the chief had texted her and found herself surrounded by towering trees and lush gardens, hiding a long and narrow cobblestone pathway that led to Geoffrey Thorne's secluded estate. Angela took a deep breath as she stepped out of the car, the scent of flowers and freshly cut grass filling her nostrils. The ground crunched under Chief Helbar's boots as he climbed out of his cruiser and came to stand next to her. "Quite the place he's got here," he mused, adjusting his hat.

"I'll say," Angela agreed as she struggled to take in every aspect of the enormous property at once. "Let's hope the man on the inside is as nice as what he's got displayed on the outside." They approached the front door and rang the bell. The corresponding chime echoed across the gardens, sending a flock of birds into flight out of the trees above them before it swung open, revealing a stern-looking butler who regarded them with a steely gaze. "May I help you?"

Angela rolled her shoulders back. "Yes, we're here to speak with Mr. Geoffrey Thorne. My name is Angela Atkinson, and this is Chief Helbar. We have some questions regarding a recent piece of art he may have added to his collection."

"Very well," the butler replied, stepping aside to let them in. "Follow me."

He led them through a grand foyer and into a long hallway lined with exquisite paintings and sculptures. As they walked, Angela couldn't help but wonder whether any of them were fakes or if this was the first time he found himself tangled up in the forgery ring.

After meandering down several winding halls, they arrived at a set of ornate double doors, which the butler opened to reveal a lavishly furnished study. A distinguished-looking man with silver hair and piercing blue eyes stood near a large mahogany desk, studying an ancient-looking map hanging on the wall.

"Mr. Thorne," the butler announced, "you have visitors."

Geoffrey Thorne turned to face them, confusion coloring his expression as he took note of the chief's police vest. A hint of fear flickered in his eyes, but it disappeared so fast that Angela was half convinced she imagined it. "Officers. How may I help you?" Angela exchanged a glance with Chief Helbar before stepping forward and holding out a hand. "My name is Angela Atkinson. I'm a private investigator. This is Chief Helbar. We are looking into the recent death of Sterling Hastings and wondered whether you could tell us about your connection to him."

Geoffrey's eyes widened slightly in surprise, but he smoothed down the creases in his jacket and gestured toward a pair of plush armchairs opposite his desk. "Please, have a seat."

Thorne sank down into his own chair and rubbed his chin. "What is it you wish to know?"

Angela studied Thorne's composed demeanor. His stiff posture and narrowed gaze betrayed the fact that he wasn't inherently comfortable with their presence, and he also seemed like a man who would not take kindly to them if they were to beat around the bush. She got straight to the point. "We know you were involved in the commissioning of a specific epergne," she began.

"One that turned out to be a forgery at the latest auction where Mr. Hastings was murdered," the chief added. "What can you tell us about that?"

Thorne considered them, shifting in his seat and letting the silence permeate the air as his posture shifted. "I don't know what you're implying, but I assure you, my dealings are legitimate."

Angela leaned forward, her gaze unflinching. "Mr. Thorne, we have evidence suggesting otherwise. It's in your best interest to be transparent with us."

The chief's tone hardened. "Withholding information now could lead to charges of obstruction of justice. But, if you cooperate, I can discuss your situation with the District Attorney. Perhaps arrange for leniency."

Thorne's eyes flickered between the two of them as he weighed his options before letting out a long sigh.

"It's true I collaborated with Conrad on that project. He contacted Penny Bedingfield to create the epergne, and I arranged for the real one, which belonged to the company that owns my gallery, to be transported here. The plan was for Conrad to exchange the fake for the real one at my gallery, along with a considerable sum of money."

The chief hummed. "And were you involved with Sterling's death?"

Thorne's face contorted and lost a good deal of its color. "Absolutely not," he exclaimed, shaking his head vehemently. "I had no reason to want Sterling dead. Our business arrangement was mutually beneficial. Penny is the one you should be questioning."

The chief nodded, though his expression was unreadable. "Thank you for your cooperation, Mr. Thorne. I stand by what I said before, but given what you've told us, we'll need to conduct a more thorough investigation into your involvement with the forgery ring. We'll need you to come downtown for further questioning."

The drive to the station was tense. Thorne sat in the back of the chief's cruiser; Angela had allowed Ruff to sit in the back just to ensure Thorne didn't try anything, and the border collie never once allowed his gaze to leave their potential perp. He sniffed the air and could practically feel the nerves radiating off him, becoming more and more potent the closer they drew to the station. *You're not telling the whole truth, are you?*

The chief, glancing at them through the rearview mirror, grunted when his gaze met Ruff's. "Never thought I'd have a collie as my backup," he joked, attempting a small smile.

Thorne, who had been staring out the window, turned slightly to look at Ruff. "He seems... well-trained," Thorne laughed feebly, even as he crossed his arms and shifted that much closer to the window.

"You could say that," Angela smirked, "Then again, you haven't seen him with my chickens."

Hey! Ruff tilted his head, letting out a soft indignant growl that nearly made Thorne jump out of his skin. "Oh, you have chickens?" Throne asked, stroking the back of his neck as he regained his composure.

Angela chuckled at Ruff's reaction, turning slightly in her seat to more fully face Thorne. "Yeah, I've got a few chickens. They keep Ruff here on his toes. Or rather, Ruff keeps them in line."

Chief Helbar let out a hearty laugh as he maneuvered the cruiser into the station parking lot. "You've got a regular zoo up there now," he put in. "Next, you'll be telling us you've taken up knitting and baking pies."

Angela rolled her eyes playfully. "Don't give me ideas, Chief. I think I had enough pies after the Gobbler Cookoff," she elbowed him in the ribs as her mind wandered to the pumpkin pie she'd been trying too hard to perfect for this past Thanksgiving. Spoiler: she'd failed miserably, but her newly acquired interest in cooking had proved invaluable in her last case. "And as much as my mother would like to think otherwise, my knitting skills are questionable at best."

Helbar snorted as he parked the cruiser. "I'll take my chances with the scarf, but I think I'll pass on any sweets."

As the car came to a stop, Angela glanced back at Thorne, who still seemed to be wound tighter than a wind-up toy.

"Alright, Thorne, let's get going. Remember, the more you can tell us, the easier this will be for everyone."

Thorne nodded, resigned, as Ruff hopped out of the car and the foursome made their way to the station. A few minutes later, Angela and Kim stood a few feet from one another as they stared intently down at Thorne. Sweat glistened from his forehead under the glare of the fluorescent lights.

"Let's start from the beginning, Mr. Thorne," Kim began, as she rested her hands on the table. "How did you first get involved with Sterling and this forgery operation?"

Thorne shifted in his seat, his gaze flitting between Angela and Kim. "It was purely business at first," he insisted. There was an edge of disdain in his voice as he crossed his arms over his chest and fixed them both with a stern glare. "Sterling approached me with an offer. I didn't know the extent of what he was involved in."

Kim leaned forward, her eyes sharp as her voice dropped to a hissing whisper. "But you eventually became aware of the forgeries?"

"I... yes, eventually," Thorne admitted, swallowing hard. "But I was in too deep by then. I thought I could manage the situation." the man averted his gaze and let out a weary sigh. "There were rumors of a mole, but I don't have any leads," he continued.

"Fair enough, but you must have suspicions," Angela pressed. "Did you ever suspect who it might be?"

Thorne shook his head and pressed his lips into a firm line. "No. It was just whispers, nothing concrete. I didn't pay it much mind, to be honest."

He cleared his throat and ran a hand through his hair. "Like I told the chief, I'm not the one that matters here. Penny worked with Sterling long before I did. Do you want answers? Ask her."

Angela and Kim exchanged a pointed glance. Clearly, they weren't going to get much more out of him, but at the same time, Angela couldn't help but wonder why Mr. Thorne seemed so insistent on pushing them toward Penny.

"You seem pretty certain about Mrs. Bedford's involvement," she mused. "Are you sure there's nothing more you can tell us?"

Thorne shook his head, his lips pressed into a thin line. The confidence he had shown earlier seemed to wane, replaced by a visible reluctance as his shoulders hunched. "Look, whatever Penny may or may not have told me, it was in confidence. Whatever she thought Conrad was going to do with the forgery, it wasn't my business. I was just there to get paid." he threw up his hands at the end of the last sentence. His chair scrapped across the floor as he pushed away from the table and shoved to his feet. "Are we done here?"

Angela and Kim exchanged a brief, knowing look. They had gleaned as much as they could from Thorne for the moment. There was no use in pressing him further.

"Yes, Mr. Thorne, we're done for now," Angela spoke first. "But don't leave town. We're still going to need to open an official investigation into your collections, and we might have more questions later."

Officer Townsend came in and escorted Thorne out of the interrogation room. Angela and Kim remained seated, contemplating everything they'd heard.

"Do you think he's telling the truth?" Kim asked once their suspect was out of earshot.

Angela frowned as she combed a lock of hair behind her ear. "I think he's telling part of it. To get the rest, well," she shrugged. "We're going to have to follow his lead and hope Penny will cooperate."

Chapter 17

Angela mulled over Thorne's words as they drove back to Penny's studio. His story seemed plausible, but there was still something nagging at the back of her mind.

"What's on your mind, Angela?" Chief Helbar asked as they rounded another bend.

"Something doesn't add up," she murmured. "Why would Conrad go so far to get the epergne if he already had a valuable forgery? What was so special about the real one?"

"That's a good question," the chief mused. "Hopefully, Penny can help us find that answer."

"Let's hope so."

"Hello again, Miss Atkinson, Chief Helbar," Penny greeted as they made their way inside. She was expecting them this time because the chief had called ahead, but she still fiddled with her hands, and she was considerably paler than the last time Angela had seen her. "What can I do for you?"

"We know Conrad commissioned the epergne from you," Angela said. "All we wanna know is why." Penny's eyes widened before she composed herself.

"H-how did you—I don't know what you're talking about."

"Miss Bedingfield," the chief said smoothly. "We're not here for you—unless you give us a reason to be." He raised a pointed eyebrow as his eyes wandered toward a table housing an unfinished project.

"OK, it's true." Penny's words trembled as she exhaled a shaky breath. "But I didn't know what he planned to do with it. I just did what he asked for."

"Did he ever mention why he was so interested in the epergne?" Angela pressed as she leaned forward.

Penny shook her head and brushed some hair out of her eyes. "No, he never said. But he was very specific about the details and seemed anxious about getting it right."

"Interesting…"

Penny nodded. "He called me constantly during the days leading up to the auction. He was terrified that someone would recognize the epergne as a forgery."

Chief Helbar exchanged a significant look with Angela. "Did he ever mention why?"

Penny shook her head. "No, he never gave any specifics. Just that it was crucial no one caught on."

Angela absently scratched Ruff behind his ears. "Chief," she intoned. "What if… the epergne at the auction was meant to be the real one? Conrad could have planned to switch them but failed, then hired Michael to steal the genuine article from Victor."

"Interesting theory," Chief Helbar mused, stroking his chin. "It would explain Conrad's anxiety about the forgery being discovered. But we won't know for sure until we find him—or Michael, for that matter."

"Right," Angela agreed as she pushed to her feet. "We need to locate either of them to get some answers."

"Thank you, Penny," Chief Helbar said as he strode toward the door to the office. "Your help has been invaluable."

"Of course." Penny's posture visibly relaxed as they made their way toward the door. "I want to put all of this behind me."

Angela nodded. "Trust me, Penny, we're going to do everything we can to help you."

***

The next day, Angela sat at her cluttered desk in her home office, struggling to see over the mounted stacks of papers. She had asked the chief to forward her everything they had on Conrad and Michael, and she'd been combing through the documents for hours with almost nothing to show for it. She ran a hand through her tousled blonde hair as her gaze flitted from one document to another, searching for something—anything—that might give them a clue as to the whereabouts of either of their vanishing suspects. As she reached for the file titled *Auction House Finds*, her phone rang, startling Ruff from where he had curled up in the sun-soaked corner of her love seat.

He glared at the offending small metal box and the unfamiliar jumble of numbers blinking up at him from the screen. *Why do humans always call when I'm trying to get some rest? Don't they know even the best dogs in crime need sleep?*

A low growl emitted from his chest, and Angela gave him a sympathetic smile. She picked up the device and held it to her ear. "Angela Atkinson, private investigator. How may I help you today?"

"Listen carefully," Angela's brows knit together. A modulator distorted the voice, and it didn't sound like anyone she recognized.

"Hello?"

"Tonight. The warehouse on Pier Road 8:30 sharp."

"I'm... I'm sorry?" Angela's pulse quickened, and her breathing rattled in her chest as she rummaged through her drawers for a pen and a nearby piece of paper. The closest thing she could find was a yellow legal pad.

"You wanna know who really killed Sterling? Show up there tonight at 8:30 on the dot for the meeting that will take place, and don't be late."

"Who is this?" Angela muttered as she scribbled down the details with a shaky hand and clenched jaw.

"If I thought it was safe to come to you, I would have," the voice replied with a scoff. "For now, this is what you get."

"Come to us?" Angela repeated. "Have you tried reaching out before?"

She was met with only a dial tone as it echoed through the office and bounced off the walls.

Ruff cocked his head to the side and whimpered. *Who was that?*

Angela's fingers were already dancing across the keypad as she called the chief.

"Hello?"

"Chief Helbar speaking."

Angela nodded, even though he couldn't see her. "Chief, I just got off a call." She leaned forward, placing her elbows on the tiny uncluttered space on the desk. "An anonymous tip about Conrad."

"Spit it out, Atkinson," Chief Helbar barked. Angela stifled a grin. That was Helbar for you. Always wanting to cut straight to the chase. "Do we have a lead?"

"Kind of." She could practically hear him frown as she leaned back in her chair.

"You're gonna have to give me more than that," he deadpanned.

"Someone called in about a meeting at the warehouse on Pier Road," she explained. "They were using a modulator, so I don't know who it was. They said if we want to know who really killed Sterling, we need to be there by eight-thirty sharp."

There was silence on the other line, but Angela could almost hear the cogs churning in the chief's mind. "Alright. I'll tell Kim and the others to prepare for a stakeout. In the meantime," he trailed off as the rustle of papers echoed through the speakers. "We've pieced together the shipping logs. Their main hub is that exact same warehouse. We think that's where the epergne is hidden."

Angela nodded. "That can't be a coincidence. Tell Kim and the others I'm coming with them."

"Alright. But be careful. I don't want any more trips to the hospital on my watch."

Angela stifled a laugh as she thought back to her last few cases. "Understood."

"Keep me posted." With that, the line went dead.

Angela hung up the phone and glanced around her office. She pulled a fresh page from her notepad along with booting up Google maps and began sketching out zones around the warehouse to map out where she thought the best vantage points would be.

"Okay, Ruff," she said when she was done. "Time for a stakeout."

Ruff allowed his tongue to loll out of his mouth. *As long as I don't have to wear that stupid vest, I'm happy.*

As they were getting ready to leave, Chief Helbar's name flashed across her screen again. "Chief?"

"Angela, we've got a snag," he grunted, bypassing any semblance of pleasantries.

"Tell me," Angela perked up as she wrapped her coat around her shoulders and grabbed Ruff's leash from the coat rack by the door.

"We think we tracked down one man who's going to be at the meeting, Walter Leighland. According to our sources, he's a very exclusive art collector with a shady past." The chief paused momentarily. "But the problem is he is from out of the country and has diplomatic immunity. Catching him is like trying to lasso a ghost."

Angela's grip on Ruff's leash tightened. Diplomatic immunity would be a tough hurdle to jump. "So, what's our play?"

"I'm gonna work with the federal authorities," Chief Helbar replied. "They've got ways around these hiccups. We're going to use their clout to cut through the red tape."

"Good," Angela nodded. "Keep me posted, Chief."

"Will do. You and Kim..." His voice softened slightly, and he blew out a long breath. "Be careful. This isn't Charlie's Hummings Hollow anymore."

"You got it, Chief." She ended the call and glanced over at Ruff. His ears perked up. *Things are getting serious.*

She smiled and reached down and scratched the scruff of his neck. "Looks like we're playing in the big leagues now, boy."

About an hour later, she entered the briefing room. Kim was already there, staring at an array of blueprints spread out on the table. She looked up at the sound of Angela's approaching footsteps, grinning when she caught sight of her.

"The chief briefed me," Kim said as she rounded the table to greet them. "I've been trying to map out a plan for tonight, but I could really use a second pair of eyes."

"Absolutely." Angela spread her own notes alongside Kim's charts. They pored over the information, double-checking angles, planning entry and exit routes, and making sure they had contingency plans for every scenario.

"Are we sure we're ready?" Angela asked as they stepped back and surveyed their work. "We can't have any screw-ups. Not with Walter's reach."

"We won't," Kim said as she squeezed Angela's shoulder and grinned. "Trust me, we got this."

A few hours later, Angela crouched behind the rusted bed of an old pickup truck, her eyes fixed on the shadowy figures moving stealthily across the warehouse's cracked pavement. Beside her, Kim's steady breathing and Ruff's rhythmic panting were the only sounds punctuating the still night air. She checked her watch as two figures drew closer to one another—Conrad and another man, presumably Walter. Eight thirty on the dot.

"Keep your eyes peeled, Kim," Angela whispered. Her gaze never wavered from the two men, silhouetted by the faint glow of a solitary streetlamp. They had no idea what was going to happen or what they were waiting for, so they had to be ready for anything.

Kim nodded, and the two of them crept closer. Angela noted the way Conrad's hands remained tucked in the pockets of his tailored coat. One bulged slightly, as if he had a hand fisted and was clutching something precious—or damning.

Walter, on the other hand, wore a superior smirk, his eyes glinting in the brief glow of the streetlights as they narrowed on Conrad like a lion stalking its prey. The constant glances Conrad kept throwing over his shoulder told her there was the only one of the two of them who seemed to enjoy these little deals.

Walter's smile grew wider as he dangled a tightly concealed leather briefcase in front of him. Conrad reached for it, a small, tightly wrapped package in his other hand as he moved in for the exchange.

"Are you sure there's no tail on you, Conrad?" Walter asked before handing it over.

Conrad nodded, his eyes darting around the barren warehouse. "I've been careful," he assured Walter as his grip tightened on the small package. "You have my word. No one knows about this meeting."

Angela and Kim strained to hear the rest of the conversation as Angela's hand rested lightly on Ruff's back. The dog stayed remarkably still, his dark eyes never leaving the suspects.

At the last second, Walter's eyes darted toward Angella's hiding spot. Ruff's tail thumped against the ground as Walter pulled back, narrowed his eyes, and whispered something unintelligible in a deep bass voice.

Conrad froze, and his face paled even in the dim light of the warehouse. Kim immediately cupped her hand around the earpiece that they were all wearing, hissing, "Chief, we've been compromised. They know we're here, and they are going to make a run for it. If we want to get him, we must move. Now!"

"I see him." Out of the corner of her eye, Angela watched as Chief Helbar's hand rose, signaling his team forward in a silent, practiced motion. They fanned out, closing the distance. Kim vaulted to her feet and darted after the rest of the team as they moved in. Conrad's head snapped up, his eyes locking onto Angela's.

"Guys, *move!* He's bolting!" she hissed.

Conrad shoved the package at Walter, who caught it midair. Immediately, he broke into a sprint as he weaved through stacks of crates with the agility of a man half his age.

"Ruff, come on!" Angela broke into a run, rounding the corner Conrad had disappeared around moments before.

"Conrad!" she yelled. "Look, we just want answers." He looked back but didn't slow.

"Chief, he's heading east toward the docks!" Angela shouted as Ruff streaked ahead of her. "Good boy. Don't let him get away."

She rounded another corner, her boots skidding on the damp cobblestone. Conrad's silhouette darted between the cones of light cast by the sporadic street lamps. Angela's breath came in sharp bursts, but she never lost sight of her target.

"Angela, he's not stopping," Kim panted through the earpiece. "We doubled back. I've got Walter detained until we can figure out how to bypass his immunity."

Conrad glanced over his shoulder and veered left, disappearing into an alley. Angela continued the pursuit but as she entered the narrow passage, she was met with nothing but the echo of her own footsteps.

"Where did you go?" She narrowed her eyes and scanned for any sign of movement as Ruff put his nose to the ground, but neither of them had any luck.

"Angela, talk to me. What's happening?" Chief Helbar's voice crackled through the earpiece.

"He's gone." Angela growled. "I don't know where." She glanced ahead of them at what appeared to be a dead end. Was it possible he had vaulted over the wall? Until tonight, she would have doubted it, but he proved himself to be much more agile than she had given him credit for.

"Let's regroup back at the warehouse. We'll figure this out," Chief Helbar said.

Angela took one last look down the desolate alley, and a long sigh escaped her. That made two failed chases in one case. She really needed to get back to the gym. "Next time, Conrad," she whispered. "You won't be so lucky."

Chapter 18

The next morning, Angela and the rest of the team met up in the briefing room of the Hummings Hollow police station. Chief Helbar stood against the back wall as Angela drummed her fingers on the table, impatient for him to begin.

"Look, everyone, I know last night was a tough break–"

"We were so close to catching him," Kim muttered. "How did he get away?"

Angela gnashed her teeth but said nothing. She knew Kim was frustrated and wasn't really blaming anyone, but she still felt guilty for letting Conrad escape.

"But just because we had a setback, it does not mean the case is over." The chief clapped his hands sharply, and it echoed through the room. "Now we need a plan. Any suggestions?"

Officer Townsend raised his hand first. "Kim and I were thinking of going back to the warehouse to see if we missed anything."

The chief nodded. "Good idea. I'm gonna check in with Jeffries and the forensics department. See if any of the results from the decanter or the other evidence we've collected have come back yet."

Murmurs went up around the room, and Angela pushed to her feet. "I was planning to go back to the auction house. See if I can go over the footage again. Maybe we missed something from that day."

The chief hummed. "OK. let me know what you find."

"Will do, Chief."

Angela headed out to her SUV and made the quick journey to the auction house. Kelly was eager to help and had no qualms about allowing Angela to see the security footage.

"Of course," she nodded after Angela explained the situation as quickly as she could. "Right this way."

Twenty minutes later, after receiving official approval from the proper channels, Angela sat in front of the monitors and studied the grainy surveillance footage with the auction house security team huddled around her. "Wait. Go back," she said, careful not to leave a fingerprint on the screen as she pointed at the top left corner. They had paused at a frame a few hours after the auction had ended, and Angela's gaze was fixated on a fuzzy individual. He had taken up residence at a table in the back of the room, and appeared to be doing much more than shipping out requested deliveries.

One man in a security uniform nodded and rewound the footage thirty seconds before the freeze frame.

"Close," Angela murmured, squinting at the corner of the screen. "But can you zoom in? I really want to see who that is in the back."

The security expert next to her tapped away at the keyboard, sharpening the edges of the image until it nearly looked like a portrait.

"There!" Angela sat forward in triumph when she recognized Conrad Cummings holding what she assumed was an imitation of the epergne. Stealthily, he made his way to the real deal.

"Got you," she whispered. But the victory was short-lived, as another figure crept in from off camera and beat him to it.

"Wait, who's that?" She squinted at the screen but couldn't make out the details. "Back it up?"

The tech guy nodded, and the footage rewound. They watched as the unknown person replaced the real epergne with another identical-looking piece and headed toward the main ballroom. Conrad barely blinked.

"Conrad was ready to switch out the original," Angela muttered to herself, "but he didn't do it in time."

Angela stood, her mind racing as she tried to piece together what that revelation meant. "Thanks, everyone. I think I've got what we need." She bid the security team farewell, then headed back to her farm to check in on Eggatha and the rest of the animals.

To her surprise, she found David already there, finishing up the last of the farm chores as she pulled her mud-splattered SUV into the driveway. An unconscious smile spread onto her lips when he waved at her from the porch steps. Angela flung open the passenger side door to let Ruff out before making her way up the steps herself, wrapping her arms around David's waist as she greeted him with a soft kiss.

"What are you doing here?" she murmured as she leaned into him, and they made their way inside. "And what smells so good?" Scents of soy sauce, sesame, and a mix of herbs wafted up her nose as they entered the kitchen.

David chuckled lightly. "Oh, it's nothing, just a little vegetable stir-fry. We've both been so busy lately that we haven't had time to see each other, so I thought I would come to surprise you."

Angela smiled as she leaned against the counter and glanced at the sizzling veggies on the stove. "Well, I appreciate it. You're a sight for sore eyes after the week I've had."

David frowned as he tore open a package of three-minute rice and shook it into a bowl before popping it in the microwave. "Uh oh. Another roadblock in the case?"

Angela hummed. "Something like that." She filled him in as quickly as she could—Michael going AWOL, the failed stakeout, and her recent breakthrough from the security tapes. "Conrad definitely meant to switch out the epergne, but I don't think that was part of the ring's plan. I think he was doing it to protect himself?"

"From Walter?"

Angela nodded, setting out two place settings while David brought the finished food over to the table, Ruff following closely behind. "From what I can figure, Walter seems to be somewhere near the top of the food chain. Townsend and Kim have him detained right now, but since he has diplomatic immunity here, we're probably going to send him back to Italy if we want to pursue prosecution."

"Can you do that?" David asked as he scooped a spoonful of rice. "I mean, do you have enough evidence?"

Angela shook her head. "Not yet. But hopefully, we will before this whole thing is over." She smiled and reached out a hand to take David's hand in hers. "But enough about my case. What have you been up to?"

They made conversation about the lessons he was teaching and the shenanigans his kids were getting into as they prepared for Christmas break, which was only a couple of weeks away. Angela designated herself as the person on dish duty that night since David had already done so much work, but that didn't stop him from trying to help. Once everything was cleaned up and they were settled in the living room, David with his nose in a book and Ruff peacefully napping at the end of the sofa while HBO played in the background, Angela decided it was time to update the chief.

She reached for her phone and punched in his number.

"Helbar here."

"Chief, it's Angela. I just wanted to update you. I think I've got something from the security footage. Do you have twenty minutes tomorrow morning?"

The chief agreed to the meeting, and the next day Angela received an email full of stills from the auction house, which she promptly forwarded to him. They gathered around his computer and Angela pointed out all the details that confirmed her theory.

"Based on these, I think Conrad was planning to pawn off the epergne to pay the loan sharks that left that note in his hotel room." She moved to the next slide, a freeze-frame of the staff member with the epergne. "But someone else got there first. Took the real epergne right from under his nose."

Chief Helbar leaned forward, his eyes narrowing as he scrutinized the image. "Makes sense. Especially since the analysis of the handwriting came back, and it looks like it might be a match not for Walter, but for someone named Chandler Redding."

Chandler... Angela made a mental note to keep an eye out for that name. "Any leads on who that might be?"

"Not yet," Chief Helbar replied regretfully. "We're doing our best to track him down, though."

Angela nodded. "I'll keep an eye out too."

"Thanks, Angela," the chief said. "In the meantime, we need to figure out what to do about our runaways. We can't touch Walter; he's protected. Conrad's slippery, and now we've got a ghost thief."

"Which is why we need to move now." Angela cut in. "We may have lost Conrad, but if we track down Michael, we can squeeze him for information. That will probably lead us to Conrad, and we can unravel this whole mess."

Chief Helbar rubbed a hand over his mustache. "Alright," he conceded. "How do you propose we do that?"

Angela's lips pursed as she thought it over. "You said you guys have been chasing him for a while, right?"

The chief grunted. "Longer than I'd care to admit."

Angela crossed her legs. "So, have you tracked his most frequent locations in the database?"

Chief Helbar scoffed. "What do you think we are, a squad of rookies?" he reported. "Of course we have."

Angela rolled her eyes and bit back a smile as Ruff shot her a quizzical look. "I had to ask, Chief," she said dryly. "And now that I know you have them, I think we should raid his last hideout."

The chief exhaled. "Angela, I know you've only been doing this for a while, but there's no way a thief as savvy as Michael would go back to his latest haunt when he knows he's being hunted. If he was that stupid, we would have caught him years ago."

Angela snickered. "I know that, chief, but we're not looking for Michael, at least not in the traditional sense."

There was a long pause on the other end of the line. "Go on."

"Look, if we keep chasing him like we have been, we're just gonna end up running after our own tails."

The chief said nothing, but Ruff tilted his head. *Hey, what's wrong with that? I love that game.*

"Even if we don't find him at his last hideout, we might still figure out what he's planning. If we do, we can beat him to the punch and track him down before his next hit."

The chief grumbled something unintelligible under his breath.

"What was that?" Angela asked as a hint of a smile quirked on the corners of her lips. If she didn't know any better, she could've sworn the chief had given her a compliment, but she couldn't be sure.

"I said you win Atkinson," he grunted. "We'll do it your way. But remember, whoever I send with you are still officers on my squad."

Angela nodded and readjusted her position on the couch. "Got it, Chief. Your squad, you're in charge. Just tell me what you need me to do."

***

"Flashbangs, check. Cuffs, check." Kim's voice was steady as she ran through her checklist. "Are we missing anything?"

"I don't think so," Angela said as she slipped on a pair of black leather gloves. She turned to see Chief Helbar strapping on his holster.

"We'll find him," he said gruffly. "And when we do, this whole rotten operation comes down."

That night, Angela gathered at the edge of town with the chief and the rest of his assembled team, including Kim and Officer Townsend. They descended on Michael's last known location - an abandoned factory, encroaching on the woods at the town's edge. The building was a large, towering brick structure, but some walls were falling apart while others were sprayed with faded lines of graffiti. Most of the windows were broken and shards of glass still lay scattered among the overgrown foliage, meaning everyone had to be extra careful where they stepped.

Angela crouched behind the wheel of the unmarked car. Her heart beat a steady rhythm against the Kevlar vest.

"Angela, you good?" Kim's voice cut through the static of the radio, and she sucked in her breath.

"Ready as I'll ever be," Angela replied. Ruff stood stiffly at her side, hackles raised beneath his vest as they waited with bated breath for the signal.

Chief Helbar's flashlight sliced through the darkness, illuminating a dirt-riddled, early faded path that led toward the shack, and Angela braced herself as they surged forward. "All right, boy," she whispered as Ruff fell into step beside her, "Let's go."

They burst into the old building, and Angela scanned the first room. Rusted machinery lay scattered across almost every inch of the floor, the steeliness punctured by only a few of the barest pieces of furniture. There was a couch that looked like it had barely any stuffing left, a wooden table missing a leg, and a lone chair right near yet another shattered window. The walls were peeling and damp, and the air was heavy with the scent of mold and decay.

"Watch for tripwires," Angela warned as they crept forward, kicking up clouds of dust as they went. "Michael's been at this so long for a reason. There's no telling what he's got in here."

"Clear left," Kim called out from the second room that had once been used for storage, now littered with broken crates and heaps of old fabric.

"Clear this way too," hissed Officer Townsend from the last of the three rooms on the first floor. It might have been an office, judging by the skeletal remains of desks and filing cabinets, their contents long since pilfered or decayed. "What now?"

"Upstairs," Helbar whispered, gesturing toward the rickety staircase when they cleared the first floor. The stairs creaked under their weight, leading to a single door at the end of the hall. It gave way with a swift kick from Townsend, and everyone spread out.

"Here," Kim spoke first, and Angela turned to see her holding up a clear bag containing a smudged print lifted from a dusty windowpane. "I'll bet that'll match Michael's prints from the database."

"Good work, Kim," Helbar grunted.

"Check this out." Angela beckoned them over to a cluttered desk where a grainy surveillance still from Victor's store was pinned under a coffee mug. "That's Michael in the background, the day before the theft."

The chief nodded. "Certainly looks like him, but I haven't seen any sign of the epergne. You?"

Officer Townsend shook his head, followed by Kim and Jefferies. "Nope, nothing yet."

Ruff nudged something on the corner of the desk, letting out a soft bark that caught Angela's attention. "Chief, look at this."

There was a map of Hummings Hollow with a series of red pins on it. The hotel, the auction house, the meeting with Walter...

"This is every place Conrad has been to recently." Kim mused, leaning over the map. "Michael was tracking him."

"Conrad skipped town with the epergne... and Michael was hot on his heels," Townsend added.

"That seems to be the case," the chief conceded. "But that still doesn't bring us any closer to either of them."

"Wait, what's this?" Angela's fingers brushed over the cold plastic of a burner phone left atop a stack of old newspapers. The tiny screen blinked with an unread voicemail icon. She beckoned the police officers over and held her breath as she pressed play.

"Michael, it's Conrad. I know you're trying to find me, but I suggest you don't. You'll get another job. This was my only way out. If you come after me, you won't like the consequences." A dial tone echoed through the room as everyone exchanged significant glances.

Angela tapped the burner phone against her palm. "You were right, Townsend," she said softly. "It seems our thief has turned into a hunter."

"Which means he's desperate," Kim added. "Desperate people make mistakes."

Angela hummed. "We just have to be patient. Watch and wait. One of them will mess up, eventually. And when they do..." she trailed off, and the officers nodded.

"Assuming neither of them ends up staring down the wrong end of a barrel before that happens," Chief Helbar grumbled. "These loan sharks aren't known for their patience or forgiveness."

"Let's keep an eye on the pawnshops and black markets," Angela said. "The epergne could surface there if Conrad gets desperate enough. Until then, all we can do is wait."

Chapter 19

Twelve hours later, Angela stepped out of her SUV, the gravel crunching underfoot as she made her way up the familiar path to her parent's retirement community. Her father was waiting in the seating area on their small front porch and Angela felt some of her stress melt away as Charlie looked up from his dog-eared mystery novel, smiling as he pushed to his feet and wrapped her in a smothering bear hug only a dad could give. "You look like you've been chasing wild geese again," he grinned when they separated. "Case stalled?"

Angela sighed, taking a seat beside him on the creaky swing bench while Ruff promptly jumped up between them. She brushed a stray blonde lock behind her ear and leaned back. "Michael and Conrad are still missing. It's like they vanished into thin air."

"Any leads at all?" Charlie closed his book with a soft thump and set it aside.

"Nothing concrete." Angela shook her head. "No matter what we do, it feels like they are always two steps ahead." She let out a long breath and absentmindedly stroked Ruff's soft fur. "We think Conrad may have taken the epergne to clear his debts. Michael took off to chase after him."

"Debts can make a man desperate," Charlie agreed. "And desperation can be dangerous. Be careful, Angie."

Angela offered a small smile, "I'm always careful, Dad. Besides, I've got Ruff and Chief Helbar looking out for me."

"Herold Helbar is as stubborn as an old mule." Charlie laughed. "Just don't give him too many gray hairs before he retires, alright?"

"Wouldn't dream of it," Angela promised, standing up from the bench and stretching. "Where's Mom?"

Just then, the front door creaked gently as it swung open. Angela turned to see her mother, Abigail, stepping out onto the porch with a mahogany music box in her hands.

"Oh Angie, you're here. Good! I was just about to ask your father where I should put this, but you have much better taste."

"Hey!" her father protested.

Angela laughed as she studied the object in her mother's hands. "Is that a... music box?" she asked.

Her mother nodded.

"Where did you get it?" Angela leaned in to admire the intricate inlay on the lid—a floral design with vines that seemed to dance around a central, ornate rose.

"From Victor's shop," Abigail replied, carefully placing it on the small wicker table in front of the porch swing. "I went into town last week, remember? It was one of my good days."

Angela nodded. She reached out and her fingers skimmed over the smooth wood before lifting the lid as the first notes of a classical piano number flittered through the air.

"Victor gave it to me. I wanted this exquisite teapot I had seen in the window, but he said it had been returned to its rightful owner." Abigail explained. "He felt so terrible about the mix-up, he let me have this instead."

"Quite the trade," Angela mused. As the melody played, she watched her mother's face soften.

"Wait until you see this," Abigail said as she fiddled with the box. Her slender fingers worked their way along the edge of the box, pressing gently until a nearly imperceptible click sounded. A hidden compartment popped open, embedded in one carving on the side.

"Wow, Mom, that's clever." Angela laughed.

"Isn't it just?" Abigail beamed, retrieving a small photograph from within the secret space. It was a family portrait taken last Christmas. "I thought it would be the perfect place to keep this."

"It sure is," Angela agreed. As she studied the photo, a new thought occurred to her. "Mom," Angela began, "That teapot you wanted. Did it have any... special features?"

Abigail paused. "Well, it had a rather intricate design around the lid. Nice bit of decoration."

"Decoration," Angela repeated. Her gaze narrowed slightly. What if the music box wasn't the only thing that had hidden compartments?

"It's beautiful, truly. Hold on to that photo, okay?" Angela gave her mother's shoulder a gentle squeeze before reaching for her phone.

"Sure, Angie. Is everything alright?"

"Everything's fine, Mom. Just need to follow up on something."

She stepped away, thumbing Kim's contact on her phone and lifting it to her ear as the porch's wooden boards creaked under her feet. The breeze nipped at her cheeks, but Angela barely noticed.

"Hello?" Kim answered.

"Kim, it's Angela. Remember the decanter in Sterling's suite? I need you to get it for me, ASAP."

"Is there a new lead?"

"Potentially. There might be a hidden compartment. Check the lid, the base, and anywhere it could be concealed. And be careful; it could be poisoned."

"Say no more." She cut her off. "I'm on it."

"Thanks, Kim. I'll be down at the station as soon as I can. First, I must check in on the antique shop." Angela ended the call and turned back to her parents with an apologetic smile. "I'm sorry, guys. I wish I could stay longer, but thank you so much." She kissed her dad first, then her mom.

The laugh line for father's eyes creased as he grinned at her. "Well, I don't know what just went down, but I'm glad we could help." He wrapped her in a one-armed hug and kissed her forehead.

***

Angela stepped into Hummings Hollow Antiques, greeted by the familiar chime of the bell above the door. As she made her way through the aisles of aged furniture and glassware, her gaze landed on Victor Callahan, who chuckled as he noticed Angela. "Angela! There you are. I was really looking forward to you pestering me again."

Ruff yipped, and Angela raised a brow. Was that a... joke? She couldn't recall the last time she heard the curmudgeonly owner try to be humorous, at least when it wasn't at her expense. She smiled thinly as he asked, "To what do I owe this pleasure?"

Angela moved toward the back of the shop and rested her hands on the counter. "My mother mentioned that the teapot was returned to its rightful owner," she replied as she scanned the back shelves for any new items. "I just wanted to know how it went."

Victor leaned against the counter, his face breaking into a rare smile that crinkled the age lines around his eyes. "Ah, the teapot saga. I located the woman, Anna, by diving into some of my old records. Found her living near the edge of town."

Angela raised a brow. "Oh really? What did she say when you gave it back?"

Victor's grin grew that much wider. "You should've seen her face," he said with a light laugh. "Turned out, the numbers scribbled in that note from her grandmother were the code to a safety deposit box. It hosted a will that had been lost and sought after for at least a generation."

Angela's eyes widened. "Oh, that's wonderful."

Victor nodded. "Indeed, it is," he sighed as his gaze wandered around the shop. "You know, it reminded me why I love this business. The items we have here are more than just objects. They're pieces of history. And sometimes, if we're lucky, they even help bring people together."

"Thanks for telling me, Victor. It's nice to see something positive come from all this," Angela said. Ruff panted in agreement and nodded.

Victor shrugged, a faint smile still playing on his lips. "Just doing my part. Now, is there anything else I can help you with while you're here?"

Angela shook her head, still processing the story of the teapot. "No, I think I'm OK," she replied. "Oh, but I did want to thank you."

"Thank me?" Victor repeated as he raised his eyebrows and tipped his head to the side, his eyes scrunching behind his glasses. "For what?"

"For the teapot... and the raccoon," Angela replied with a bemused grin. "They gave me an idea. I might be one step closer to solving my mystery, thanks to what I found here."

As they spoke, Ruff perked up, his gaze fixed on something near the display window. Angela followed his line of sight and couldn't help but laugh. There, amidst the antiques, was the raccoon again, fiddling with the hands on an ornate cuckoo clock.

"I thought you were going to call the exterminator," Angela said with a chuckle as she arched an eyebrow.

Victor offered a wry smile as he stuffed his hands in his pockets and glanced at the display window. "I changed my mind. The little guy has become quite fond of my antiques. Believe it or not, he's helping to draw customers. He seems to have a knack for highlighting items that have been languishing in the back of my shop for far too long."

Angela chuckled, watching as the raccoon leap through the maze of antiques. "Well, I suppose every antique shop could use a mascot like that."

The raccoon stopped and swiveled to look at them. *Who me?* It seemed to ask. Its eyes glinted with a mischievous intelligence and it winked in Victor's direction before it scampered away, disappearing behind a row of old books.

"Take care, Victor. And thanks again," Angela said, smiled as she and Ruff headed for the door.

They drove to the station as fast as she could while still staying within the speed limit and got there just in time to see Kim set the decanter down on the scuffed top of her desk. The room was quiet, save for the hum of an old air conditioner. Ruff trotted next to her and perked up at the sight of Kim.

"Found it exactly where you said," Kim watched as Angela rotated the decanter carefully.

"Thanks, Kim." Angela's gaze narrowed as she examined the intricate patterns etched into the crystal. "The craftsmanship is impeccable." She felt a slight give in the lid, and her pulse quickened.

"Ah-ha!" She fiddled with the seemingly solid top until a subtle click rewarded her efforts. A small compartment within the lid revealed itself.

"Would you look at that?" Kim leaned in closer, her brown eyes wide. "What do you think is inside?"

"Only one way to find out." Angela retrieved a pair of tweezers from her jacket pocket and carefully extracted a tiny glass vial filled with clear liquid from the cavity.

"I'll bet you anything this is poison," Angela said, holding the vial up to the light.

Kim nodded and punched it between her fingers. "I'll bet you're right. If so, we take no chances. This needs to go to forensics right away."

"Agreed," Angela said. "Keep it under wraps, though. Tell the chief of course, but we don't want word getting out before we know what we're dealing with."

"Understood." Kim gave a mock salute, and Angela's lips twitched into a small smile.

With Ruff at her heels, Angela walked toward her SUV. But she didn't get very close before—

"Wait!" She turned to see Kim jogging to catch up, presumably coming back from dropping the vial with forensics. "Where do you think you're off to in such a hurry?"

Angela didn't break stride. "Back to the warehouse. Chief said it was one of the bases for the op. If that's true, there's got to be something we missed—a clue to where Michael and Conrad are holed up. If we're right about what's in that vial, then I'm almost certain Conrad murdered Sterling. But we can't convict him without a confession."

Kim frowned. "You're not seriously considering going there alone, are you? Not with everything we've found, and two criminals on the loose?"

"Ruff is with me," Angela replied, patting her side where the loyal dog kept pace.

Kim gave her a long look, and she smirked. In truth, Angela knew her friend's concern wasn't unfounded; the warehouse was isolated, and if either Conrad or Michael were there, things could get dangerous quickly.

"I'm not letting you go play hero by yourself." Kim fell into step beside her as they continued toward the SUV. "I'm coming with you."

Angela nodded. Her father had told her to be careful and having a backup wouldn't hurt. "Alright, thanks, Kim."

"Let's just be careful, okay? You end up in the hospital again, on my watch, and I'm pretty sure the chief will put my head on the chopping block."

Angela laughed and nudged her shoulder. "Come on. Helbar wouldn't do that. He loves you."

Kim snorted. "Yeah, well, your dad was his old partner. So even if you technically don't work here, I'm pretty sure you have more clout than me."

"Careful is my middle name," Angela joked with a twinkle in her eye.

Uh, really? Ruff barked in protest and gave her a pointed look, which she completely ignored.

They climbed into the SUV and Ruff settled into the backseat with a sigh. Angela turned the key in the ignition, the engine roared to life,

The drive to the warehouse was quiet, except for the jingle of Ruff's collar and the screech of tires on asphalt. When the building came into view, Angela braced herself.

"Ready?" She cut the engine and looked over at Kim.

"Always."

Kim's flashlight beam swept across dusty shelves and abandoned crates as they entered the warehouse. Ruff trotted beside her, his nose skimming every surface as he searched for anything out of place. *It smells like mothballs in here. Mothballs and...* he sniffed again, *stress.*

"Check these out," Angela murmured, pointing at a stack of weathered boxes. Kim nodded, flipping open lids as gently as she could. They checked every corner and crevice, but Angela wasn't sure what they were looking for. The air was stale, thick with stones, and a long history of secrets.

"Nothing here," Kim said as she slumped against the wall and ran a hand down her face. "Ugh. It feels like we're chasing ghosts."

"Keep looking," Angela replied.

They moved further into the warehouse and Angela's fingers brushed against the coarse tops of the crates until they snagged on a sliver of paper sticking out from a concealed slot beneath the surface.

"Got something," she called out.

Kim hurried over, training her light on the box as they worried together to pry it open. When they finally removed the lid, they found stacks upon stacks of documents. They were brittle and yellowed, but some of the writing was still legible. Angela's pulse quickened as she scanned the contents, recognizing the emblem at the top—the Hummings Hollow Hope Foundation.

"Wait... my mom has supported this charity before," Angela said softly.

Kim hummed. "Maybe there's more to it than goodwill and bake sales."

"Looks like it."

"Let's take these back to your office," Kim suggested as she scooped up the top files. "Maybe the chief knows something."

"Agreed." Angela picked up a few more files and tucked them in her jacket. "Ruff, heel," Angela commanded gently. He barked and fell into step beside her as they made their way back to the car.

***

In her office, Angela perched on the edge of her desk, her features bathed in the glaring glow of her laptop. She sifted through the digital maze of bank statements and emails for anything she could find on the Hummings Hollow Hope Foundation. Her fingers danced over the keys, following the trail of donations that snaked from the charity into a thicket of shell companies.

"Look at this," she murmured, zooming in on a series of transactions and tilting the monitor toward Kim, who stood behind her.

"Whoever this Chandler is has been busy," Kim noted, pointing at the screen where his name appeared alongside hefty sums. "And so has Walter."

Angela nodded. "Tomorrow, I'll talk to Mr. Landon. It looks like he's the head of the charity; he might know what's going on."

"Or he could just be a pawn in Walter's game," Kim countered.

Angela nodded as she rested her chin on her hand. "Either way, we need to find out."

***

The next day found Angela standing in the modest headquarters of the Hummings Hollow Hope Foundation. The walls were covered with photos of community events and smiling volunteers.

"Mr. Landon," Angela rested her hands on the back of the chair opposite the charity director's desk. "Thank you for meeting me." She rounded the chair to take a seat and dropped some copies of the financial records she had made from her search yesterday. "I've come across some concerning financial records. They appear to be linked to your company and I—" she inhaled deeply and folded her hands in her lap. "I need to know what you can tell me about them."

"Surely there's been some mistake," he stammered.

"I wish there was," Angela said. "But money trails don't lie," she retorted sharply. "And neither do forged antiques that somehow end up in your silent auctions."

The director's face paled and his hands trembled slightly as they rested on his cluttered desk. "That's a serious claim. What proof do you have?"

"Enough to know Conrad Cummings and someone named Walter funneled money through the foundation." Angela watched him closely, and a flicker of recognition passed over his features. He swallowed hard, his fingers fidgeting with a pen that suddenly seemed foreign in his hand. "We thought we were doing good. We didn't know…"

"Didn't know, or didn't want to know?" Angela challenged. The temperature in the room dropped a few degrees.

"Please, Ms. Atkinson, our reputation—"

"Reputations should be earned," Angela interjected. "Hummings Hollow deserves better. I know you know that."

The man deflated. He opened his mouth, closed it, and ran a hand down his face. Then, finally, he spoke. "Conrad was… persuasive," Mr. Landon said after a long silence. He looked away and his shoulders slumped as he sat forward. "He assured me it was all genuine. I never imagined—"

"And Sterling Hastings?" Angela asked. "Does that name mean anything to you?"

"Hastings?" He hesitated, then sighed, the fight draining from him. "Conrad mentioned him once or twice. Seemed kind of afraid of him. Said he had more pull than he should have …"

"Did you ever push him for more information?" Angela pressed.

The director shrugged. "I tried, but he was always vague." He let out a long breath as he shifted through the files Angela had laid out. "I wish I would've known sooner. If I had, I would've gone straight to the police. This isn't what our foundation is about." His voice cracked, and Angela offered him a sympathetic smile as she pushed to her feet. "Thank you for your time, Mr. Landon. Come on boy, let's go." His ears perked up, and they walked out into the crisp winter air.

No sooner had they rounded the corner than Angela's phone vibrated in her pocket. She pulled it out to see Kim's name flashing on the screen. "Hey, what's up?"

"Angela," Kim's voice was tight, and it held a tint of urgency that made Angela's stomach flip. "There's been a break-in at your place. How soon can you get home?

"Oh, my goodness," Angela muttered under her breath, her heart thudding unevenly. "Any idea who it might be?"

"No sign of 'em now. But you need to get here fast. We've secured the scene."

"Thanks, Kim." Angela broke into a jog as she felt the color drain from her face. Ruff kept pace beside her.

"I'm on my way."

Chapter 20

The drive home was a blur. The countryside rolled past her window, and her thoughts raced alongside the roar of the engine. Who robbed her? Better yet, what did they take? Angela could at least take comfort that whoever it was hadn't harmed any of her animals. Kim would've told her if that was the case. But if they took what she thought they did...

"Stay focused," she murmured, shaking the thought away and gripping the steering wheel until her knuckles turned white. "You've faced worse."

She swung into the driveway, gravel spraying beneath her tires. The sight of uniformed officers and the familiar outline of Chief Helbar's cruiser did nothing to ease the tightness in her chest. She parked haphazardly and jumped out, Ruff on her heels as her gaze swept over the property. From the outside, everything seemed normal, but she had a sinking feeling the inside would be a very different story.

"Angela!" Kim jogged toward her, a wave of concern contorting her features despite the professionalism of her uniform. "We're still clearing the rooms, but it looks like they were searching for something specific."

"Or someone trying to send a message," Angela replied as she moved toward the farmhouse.

They stepped over the threshold, and she held back a gasp as they scanned the disarray that was once her orderly living room. The soft glow of the late afternoon sun filtered through the windows, illuminating overturned furniture. Pillows had been torn apart, their stuffing strewn all across the carpet. The couch was no longer a functional piece of furniture. Instead, its cushions had been flung across the room with only one landing right side up. Her bookshelves were nearly empty, their contents scattered across the rest of the house. Angela made her way down the hall to her makeshift home office, not surprised at all at the chaos that greeted her. Every drawer had been yanked open, their contents clinging to the edges or flung across her desk, loveseat, printer, and every available surface in a careless rush.

"Easy does it," she whispered. She pulled her phone from her pocket and started snapping photos of everything she could find, both for her own reference and for the chief's. As she moved, her footsteps shuffled along the carpet, but a sudden crunch of shattered glass broke through the eerie silence. She bent down, carefully plucking a jagged piece from the ground—its sharp edges catching the light, throwing prisms onto the wall. Her gaze moved to the window and sure enough, there was a gaping hole that was visible between the curtains.

"Angela? Is that you?" Chief Helbar's voice echoed from down the hall, and he approached and then lingered in the doorway. A frown creaked his stern features, intensifying the line in his face as he held up an evidence bag containing a small pendant of a phoenix.

"Glad to see you're OK. We're still canvassing the scene, but I found this. Does it mean anything to you?"

Angela straightened up, brows furrowed as she tried to place where she'd seen it before. Then her eyes widened. She walked over and crinkled the edge of the bag in her fingers. "Actually, yeah. I think Michael was wearing this when my dad and I tried to chase him down." She glanced back toward her disheveled office and a chill ran down her spine. What if he took the evidence files?

The chief grunted and rubbed the ends of his mustache. "Seems our phantom thief has reappeared," he said. "And got away again."

"May I?" Angela reached out, her fingers brushing against the plastic as she inspected the pendant. It was unmistakable—the intricate design, the colorful feathers–it was the same one she had seen at the auction, and during the chase.

"Found it by the back door," the chief continued. "Almost like he dropped it on his way out."

Ruff growled in displeasure as he recognized the scent on the pendant. *He better not run into me again.*

"Or left it as a signature," Angela mused. Michael knew they were chasing him. Maybe he was feeling cocky after swiping those files and...

The chief raised an eyebrow. "You think he's taunting us?"

"Maybe." Angela handed the bag back to him.

"Either way, we've got our work cut out for us." The chief tucked the evidence bag into his coat pocket and gestured toward the chaos. "Let's go over to the warehouse again. See if we missed anything else."

Just then, the door burst open, and Angela and the chief swiveled toward the sound.

"Angela!" Charlie called out.

"In here," she yelled back, stepping into the hall.

"Honey, are you alright?" her father sprinted toward the office and relief spread across his face when his gaze landed on hers.

"I'm fine, Dad," she assured him as he wrapped his arms around her and squeezed until she could barely breathe. "It was my stuff that took the hit, not me."

"This time," her father admonished lightly, quirking a brow. "It could've been so much worse. What if you had been at home?" Angela rolled her eyes but leaned into her father's hug. When she first became a PI, she thought her father's years of experience on the force would make him a little less... smothering. Yes, she had put herself in danger more than once—more than a few times, actually—in the name of a case, but she thought he of all people would understand. After all, he had done the same thing for most of her childhood.

But oh, how wrong she was.

"You may be an adult now, Angie," he told her once. "But no matter what, you'll always be my little girl."

"Angie!" David burst into the room a second later and Angela felt another wave of tension leave her as she caught sight of her boyfriend, and her father allowed him to join in on the hug. "Oh, I was so worried!"

Hey, don't forget about me! Ruff barked and nudged his way into the circle and all three of them started laughing, despite the situation.

"You weren't the only one," Angela said as she bent down to scratch behind Ruff's ears. "But I'm fine. You don't have to worry so much."

Her father squeezed her shoulder. "Honey, that's never gonna happen. You may be a private investigator now, but that doesn't mean your family is ever going to stop worrying. In fact, it means we're gonna worry even more than normal."

Angela shook her head but let the matter go, in lieu of any more protests.

Kim, who had previously stepped away to coordinate with Officer Townsend, walked up behind them and offered more assurance.

"She's okay. Angela's fine, and so are all the animals. No one was home when it happened."

David let out a breath and pulled her closer while her father disentangled himself from the embrace in favor of going to search for Chief Helbar, intending to join him to canvas the rest of the house. Angela smiled. Even though her father was no longer a cop anymore, she suspected the itch to solve a case never quite went away. Especially when it came to family.

Meanwhile, Angela entwined her hands with David's, and the two of them wandered to the front yard, stopping by the chicken coop to check in on Eggatha and her two chicks Indy and Christi.

"I can't believe he broke into my house," Angela murmured.

"We'll make sure this doesn't happen again," David promised. "I'm just glad you're safe."

Chapter 21

B ack inside, Angela watched as her father and Chief Helbar moved through each
room. Despite a thorough investigation, the police found no other leads, other than
confirming that Angela was right. Michael had taken the evidence files from her office.
Luckily, they weren't her only copies.

The next day, her shoes echoed against the polished floor of the auction house. She
brushed a loose strand of blonde hair from her face and made sure Ruff was pressed
against her as she approached the gleaming reception desk.

"Hello again, Kelly," Angela said, waving at the secretary that had been nothing but
helpful thus far. "Could I see the records from the auction again? Particularly the items
sold?"

Kelly smiled as she pushed to her feet. "Of course," she said cheerfully before disappearing into the back, returning with an embossed Manila folder. "Are you getting close
to cracking the case?"

Angela smiled as she took the folder from her. "I hope so. I just need to confirm a few
more details." She sat in a nearby chair and flipped the folder open. Her gaze darted down
the list and her eyebrows rose. The director of the foundation had been right. Sterling was
an influential man indeed. He owned more of the items than she had previously realized.
Maybe that was the reason the forgery ring had reached out to him in the first place.
Maybe he was more valuable to them than a simple showman. Thankfully, every entry
was meticulously recorded: lot numbers, item descriptions, final bids, and the identities
of those who now possessed pieces of Sterling's legacy.

"Thank you," Angela murmured. One entry stood out to her, its description a
near-perfect match to the charm that had been found at her house.

"Gotcha," she whispered to herself, tracing his name. Michael Dunford. So, she was right; he had been there, right under their noses this entire time. She glanced at the buyer list again, noting an avid collector named Jorgensen, who had purchased half a dozen of Sterling's previously owned pieces. Perhaps interviewing him would be a good place to start.

Angela reached for her phone and punched in the number listed under his contact. The line clicked, and a gruff, businesslike voice greeted her on the other end. "If you're selling something, I don't want it."

"Mr. Jorgenson? This is Angela Atkinson. I'm a private investigator looking into some matters regarding Sterling Hastings. I noticed you were quite the avid buyer at his last auction, and I would love to talk to you about taking some of those pieces off your hands."

"They're not for sale," he said tersely.

Angela leaned back in her chair. "Everything has a price," she said simply. "Please, Mr. Jorgenson, I just want to talk. Say the Lake House in an hour?"

A prolonged silence lingered on the other end of the phone before the man finally sighed. "All right, you have one hour, but not a minute longer. And the price better be good."

Angela smiled. "Thank you. I'll see you there."

An hour later, Angela leaned forward at the weathered picnic table outside the Lake House, her blue eyes fixed on the man sitting across from her. She set down her coffee cup and folded her hands atop the table, studying his stiff posture. He was an earnest-looking man with spectacles sliding down his nose. Honestly, he looked much more like a friendly history professor instead of the ruthless dealer she had corresponded with on the phone.

"Mr. Jorgenson," Angela began, her tone casual yet insistent, "thank you so much for meeting me here—"

"I don't have time for pleasantries," the man snapped as he placed his list of collectibles between them on the table. "Do you have an offer for me or not?"

Angela smiled and sat back. She had to give the man credit. He didn't enjoy beating around the bush. "Well, unfortunately, sir, I have a bit of a confession to make. I'm not actually here to make any deals."

The man narrowed his eyes and scoffed before pushing to his feet. "Well, in that case, this meeting is over."

Angela jumped up. "No, please wait. What I told you on the phone is true. I am a private investigator, but I'm looking into more than Sterling's collection. I'm trying to find out who killed him."

The man turned around, his eyes bulging behind his glasses. "K-killed him?" he stuttered. "You mean Sterling is... dead?"

Angela studied his body language for any sign of guilt, but he looked genuinely surprised. She nodded. "I'm afraid so."

Mr. Jorgensen's mouth flopped open like a fish, and he wobbled back to the table in a kind of trance. "Wow..." he whispered. "I didn't... I mean, he seemed so confident."

"Confident?" 'Angela echoed, quivering an eyebrow. "In what way?"

Jorgenson glanced around before leaning in. "Well, it's just... he said this one would be unforgettable. That it was going to clean house."

"Clean house?" Angela repeated.

"Y-yeah," Jorgenson stammered. "He made it sound like some kind of... I don't know, sting operation? Like he was setting a trap for someone."

"Interesting." Angela tapped her finger on the table. "Did he mention anyone else involved in this plan? A partner, perhaps?"

"Sort of," Jorgenson confessed, pushing his glasses up. "I know he was working with someone, but I never got a name. Sterling was secretive and said it was someone who could help him bring down the whole ring." He swallowed hard. "When I found out he was involved in all this, I told him we should just go to the police, but he warned me not to. Said he didn't want me to get hurt." He frowned and stared into the distance. "Guess now I know why."

Angela nodded. "Thank you, Mr. Jorgenson. You've been very helpful."

After Jorgenson left, Angela drove to the police station where Chief Helbar awaited. He crossed his arms, a dubious expression etched on his face.

"Angela," he greeted gruffly. "I hope that meeting gave you something solid." She had only looped him in about ten minutes prior.

"I think so," Angela replied, outlining what Jorgenson had revealed.

"We need to dig deeper, Chief. Whoever Sterling's partner is, they may be able to help us track down the missing members."

"Alright. Let's strategize," Chief Helbar said as he ushered her into his office, cluttered with files and faded photographs of Hummings Hollow plastered along the walls.

Angela perched on the edge of a chair, her gaze flitting over the chief's extensive notes pinned to a corkboard. "We should interview the other buyers—see if anyone else caught wind of Sterling's plans or noticed any unusual behavior."

"Right. And we'll need to ask specific questions to throw them off balance and get them talking," Angela added.

"Okay. I'll arrange the interviews. You go back to your office and let me know if you find anything else."

"Will do, Chief," Angela said as she pushed to her feet.

The next day, Angela sat in the interrogation room with Kim, her elbows resting on the table that separated her from Nelson Sharpe, a jittery man with a five o'clock shadow and an oddly good poker face. The cramped room smelled faintly of stale coffee and decades-old linoleum cleaner. A single overhead light cast stark shadows, making the interviewee's features even sharper than they already were.

"Mr. Sharpe," Angela began, her voice low and soothing, "you mentioned earlier that you often received shipments from Sterling. Did he handle these personally?"

"Ah, yes, he was always very... hands-on with his deliveries." Nelson's fingers fidgeted with the hem of his tweed jacket, a thread unwinding beneath his nails.

"Interesting choice for an auctioneer," Kim mused. "Was there a particular reason he took such an interest in the shipping process?"

Nelson hesitated, glancing up before averting his eyes. "Well, it wasn't just about the shipping. He—I think he wanted to keep an eye on certain items. Confidentiality and all."

"Of course, confidentiality is key," Angela agreed, nodding. "But surely, for a man as busy as Sterling, he must have had a secure place to store such valuable pieces?"

"Uh, yes. He mentioned—no, I shouldn't say. It was supposed to be a secret," Nelson stammered, biting his lip.

"Mr. Sharpe," Kim cleared her throat and steepled her fingers. "Sterling's gone now, and we need to ensure whoever did this receives proper justice. If there's something you know..."

There was the briefest flicker of doubt in Nelson's eyes, but Angela caught it. She knew they had him.

"Alright," he whispered. "He kept talking about some storage facility within the shipping company where they stored the special items, but I never went. I don't know where it is, I swear!"

"Thank you, Mr. Sharpe. That's very helpful." Angela gave him a reassured smile.

As they escorted Nelson out, Angela's mind raced. She needed to act quickly.

"Chief," Angela announced, striding into his office with Ruff trailing behind her.

"Angela, what is it?" Chief Helbar looked up with a weary expression.

"Nelson Sharpe let it slip that Sterling was using a hidden storage facility," she said. "Apparently, he used it for special items—if he really was planning to expose the ring, who knows what else he has in there? We need to move fast before anyone catches wind that we're onto them."

"Alright," Helbar grumbled, rising from his chair with a groan. "I'll pull some strings and get a warrant to search the place. You're sure you got everything out of Sharpe?"

"Positive," she replied. "He seems to be a bystander. Jorgenson seemed like more of a friend, but neither of them knew much."

"Alright," Helbar conceded, reaching for the phone. "I'll call the DA for the warrant, then. But Angela, be careful. If this storage facility is what we think it is, you could be walking into a hornet's nest."

Angela nodded, rolling her shoulders back. "I appreciate that you care, Chief," she said, smiled softly. "But trust me, I've got this."

***

The tang of salt and rust hung heavy in the air as Angela stood at the threshold of the storage facility, Ruff pacing by her side. The gray light of early dawn seeped through the corroded metal shutters, casting an eerie glow over the maze of crates and tarp-covered shapes within. She took a cautious step forward, and Ruff growled slightly.

"Easy, boy," she murmured. His ears were pricked forward in alert, but nothing seemed out of the ordinary. Anticipation buzzed through her veins as she flicked on her flashlight and shoved the heavy door open. Angela gasped. Her flashlight beam danced across a whole auction worth of items: canvases stacked against the wall, statues with chipped noses and fake patinas, and even vases penned with signatures of long-dead artists.

Her heart raced as she uncovered yet another incriminating stack of documents—bills of sale, shipping manifests, all meticulously organized and all entirely fraudulent. The entire room was a treasure trove of evidence, but the most damning piece was nestled between two leather-bound ledgers, a small, unassuming volume inscribed with *This journal belongs to Sterling Hastings* on the front page. Angela's heart pounded in her chest as she flipped through the pages, yellowed and filled with Sterling's tight, cryptic handwriting.

Angela settled on an old steamer trunk while Ruff curled up beside her protectively and together, they cracked open the journal. The scent of aged paper and ink enveloped them both as Angela scanned the entries.

"Look at this, Ruff," she whispered as she traced the edge of a page. "References to the epergne... Conrad... Walter."

Ruff whined softly, nudging her hand with his nose. *So? What does it all mean?*

"Patience, we're getting there." Angela's eyes darted down the list of names, some familiar from the auction house, and others not so much. There was another list that seemed to include all the major players in the ring. Some were pawns, but others—she paused, squinting at the upper echelons of the list—were key players. The list wasn't just a record; it was a map leading directly to the masters of the forgery ring. Walter was at the top, just as she had expected, though she was beginning to wonder if that was his real name. Her pulse quickened. *Sterling, you clever fox, you almost had them.*

And we'll get them. Ruff's tail thumped against the trunk, his dark eyes locked onto hers. Angela nodded at him before marking the page with a folded corner and closing the journal, cradling it against her chest.

Angela chewed on the end of her pen, a habit that had carried over from her days as a waitress at the Lake House. The musty smell of old paper and dust clung to the air, mingling with the salty tang of the nearby sea. She rifled through the remaining ledgers scattered in the same box where they'd found the journal, her fingers brushing over the bumpy leather textures.

"Chandler, alias James," she murmured when his name came up for what seemed like the hundredth time. A frown creased her brow as she recalled her father's offhand comment about Penny's tumultuous past. "Wasn't he...?" She trailed off as the memory clicked into place. James was Penny's ex—the one who left town under mysterious circumstances right after the ring had targeted him. Angela's heart pounded in her chest. Did his involvement go deeper than they thought, too?

Her gaze drifted back to the journal. Ruff nudged her hand with his wet nose. *Hey, let me see!* She ruffled his ears and gave him a smile before returning her attention to the pages.

"Focus, Angela," she chided herself softly, flipping through the journal pages once more. Her eyes landed on the list of names, and she leaned in closer, analyzing each one. Only then did she notice the thin red line drawn between Walter's name and Chandler's just below it. There were some chicken scribbles in the margin, but she couldn't quite make it out.

"Walter... Chandler..." she read aloud, tapping the page as she squinted to deepen the handwriting and follow Sterling's train of thought.

One note read, *Chandler's sudden shift in behavior - too coincidental? It started right after he told Walter about Penny–which he only did because he was coerced. But why would Walter be worried about a member's dating life? Surely Chandler didn't tell her. He is smarter than that, right?*

Another scribble caught her eye. *Walter's meetings - more frequent now. He's getting antsy. Why?*

Sterling's handwriting became more erratic as Angela continued flipping through the pages. *Chandler wanted out. Told Penny. Risk to Walter's operation?* Angela's breath hitched. If Chandler had confided in Penny about wanting to leave the forgery ring, and Sterling had somehow learned of this, that was more than enough of a motive. But then, why not kill him before going underground? Why wait this long? And what about the sniper? Her father had said Chandler was the one being targeted first.

She kept reading as the pages crinkled slightly beneath her fingers. *Walter's reaction to Chandler asking him to meet Penny- protective or controlling?*

Angela frowned. What did that mean? I mean, it was true enough that Penny was an excellent forger. But if Chandler was aiming to get out the whole time, why waste time recruiting her? Better yet, why put her in Walter's line of fire at all? Angela skimmed a few more pages, and her breath caught at the last scribbled note.

Breaking: I overheard Chandler and Walter talking last night when they thought every-one had gone to bed. Walter called Chandler his son. I never even considered it because they have two last names, but everyone knows Walter's is an alias. And Chandler has had too many to count.

Angela's blood ran cold, and her heart leaped into her throat.

Did Walter have his own son targeted? Chandler disappeared three days later.

A chill ran down her spine. The idea that Walter may have organized his own son's disappearance was a level of cold calculation she had not considered. And if it was true, it meant Walter was a far more dangerous man than any of them had dared to presume.

Angela's pulse pounded in her ears as she skipped down to the bottom of the page. There, at the very bottom, circled in bright red ink, was Sterling's name, scrawled in hasty handwriting.

"Oh, my goodness," Her hands shook as they tightened around the leather binding, cracking under the pressure of her grip and she turned wide-eyed toward Ruff. "He knew he was a marked man," she whispered. "He was already living on borrowed time, which explained why he felt so comfortable attempting to take the rest of them down."

Ruff stood up a little taller and poked his nose over the bottom of the journal, but Angela held it just barely out of reach.

"Ruff, this changes everything," Angela said, straightening up. "If this is a power diagram and Chandler and Walter are at the top of this food chain..." She let the sentence hang unfinished, her mind racing. The thought of Penny being involved with the likes of them sent a shiver down her spine. Was her clever artistry being exploited by these men? Or was she an equal party in their schemes?

Ruff's ears perked up, watching her every move. *Well, what are you waiting for?* He seemed to say. *Let's go.*

Angela flipped open her notebook, the frayed edges brushing against her fingers as she contemplated Penny's role in this tangled web. She had always found Penny to be an innocent bystander who got caught in the wrong place at the wrong time, but what if she was just a well-trained actress who knew how to get people—especially the police—on her side?

The trunk creaked under her weight as she leaned forward, right before a crisp winter breeze wafted through the cracked window of the storage facility. Ruff looked up from his spot on the cool concrete floor. James, or rather, Chandler, Sterling, the auctions—Penny was the common thread, but she had seemed anything but conniving when Angela had interacted with her before.

She continued reading and her hands trembled slightly when she found an entry dated just two days before Sterling's untimely demise.

"Operation Seagull is set for the final lot," she read aloud. "If all goes well, then all of this will finally be over. If it doesn't..." she trailed off when he stopped writing.

Well, that all but confirmed it. Sterling planned a coup. And he might have succeeded, if not for Conrad and the bounty on his head. The knowledge that he was so close to succeeding fueled Angela's resolve.

"Imagine the look on their faces when the hammer came down on the truth," she mused, turning to Ruff with a mischievous grin. It wasn't often she found herself rooting for the victim, but now that she had the complete picture, she was more determined than ever to finish what he started.

As she closed the journal with a satisfying crack, Angela frowned. The spine bulged, protruding out further than the ledgers of equal size in the crate where the journal had been hidden. *What's this?* Her fingers traced the grooves in the leather, and her breath caught in her throat when she recognized a subtle irregularity in the stitching. *That's not supposed to be there.*

Angela wasn't much of a seamstress, much as her mother had tried to make it otherwise. However, she knew enough to spot that whoever had bound this journal had done so with a method different from traditional means. She looked left, then right, searching the storage room for something sharp. She found a pocket knife buried among a pile of smaller trinkets and carefully wedged it under the false thread, unraveling it with each delicate tug.

What are you doing? Ruff nudged his nose into her lap, but she gently nudged him back.

"Good boy, stay back," she said softly. He edged closer and then sat down with a soft huff, though his eyes tracked her every move.

One, two...

The last stitch gave way, and a small compartment spilled open. Angela's pulse quickened as she glimpsed the edge of a sliver of metal amidst the antiquity of leather and paper.

"Hello, what do we have here?" she whispered. Her fingers, steady despite the adrenaline flooding her system, carefully teased what appeared to be a flash drive from its hiding place. It was no larger than a postage stamp, but the feeling of the cool metal between her fingers sent a fresh current of excitement pulsing through her.

"Ruff, this could be it. This could crack the case wide open." Angela held the flash drive up to the dim light filtering through the dust-moted air of the storage facility and rolled the device between her fingertips. Evidence, names, transactions—everything they would need to take down the ring could be right at her fingertips.

I knew we'd find something. Ruff's ears perked up, and his tail thumped against the concrete floor as Angela placed the flash drive securely in her pocket.

"Let's get this to Chief Helbar."

Chapter 22

Angela's hands trembled as she slid the flash drive into her computer's USB port in her office. The soft click as it connected seemed to echo through the quiet of her farmhouse kitchen. She leaned forward and pulled her blonde hair back into a functional ponytail.

The upload of the file was torturously slow, but finally, a fresh table of folders popped up on the screen when her mouse hovered over the new disk icon. Angela's fingers danced across the keyboard, inputting the decryption code she had deciphered from Sterling's journal with the chief's help.

As she sifted through the files, rows upon rows of meticulously detailed emails and documents began to reveal the forgery ring's intricate web. It was all there: coded messages, transaction dates, falsified provenances.

Her pulse sped up when a file labeled "Confidential" caught her eye. She double-clicked and was met with grainy footage of Sterling himself, looking over his shoulder as if afraid of being watched, even in the supposed privacy of his own hotel room.

"Listen," his voice crackled, through the speakers, hoarse and tinged with terror but also not without an edge of determination. "I hope no one ever needs to find this. If you're watching this, it means…" he swallowed and fiddled with the collar of his shirt. "It means something has gone wrong. And as much as I hope it doesn't…" he shifted in his seat and his gaze darted toward the door, which was barely visible in the upper left corner of the screen, "… the evidence you need is in the safety deposit box 1027."

Angela held her breath and squinted at the screen, scrutinizing every pixel of the video for every detail. When it was over, Angela pushed away from the desk. She needed to get to that safety deposit box. And she had to act fast—who knows if Conrad or Michael had somehow followed the same trail?

She grabbed her phone and quickly dialed the chief's number.

"Chief, it's Angela," she said when he answered. "I've got a lead on the case—a safety deposit box that belonged to Sterling."

There was a brief pause on the other end before the chief responded. "Alright, Angela. I'll have Officer Townsend meet you there in half an hour with the warrant."

Exactly thirty minutes later, Angela slipped her hand into the pocket of her weather-beaten jacket, feeling for the outline of her identification. With a determined stride, she pushed through the brass-handled doors of Hummings Hollow's Community Bank.

The air inside tinged with the scent of old leather and polished wood as Angela's shoes clacked on the marble floor.

"Good afternoon," Angela offered a polite nod to the teller. Her name plate read 'Mavis'. "Morning, Ms. Atkinson," Mavis returned the greeting with a practiced smile. "What can I do for you today?"

Angela leaned in slightly, lowering her voice out of habit more than necessity. "I need access to a safety deposit box. It belonged to Sterling Hastings."

Officer Townsend stepped up behind her and handed over the warrant. "We're not family," he explained. "But we're here on police business."

"Of course," Mavis replied, not skipping a beat. "May I see your ID, please? Then I can use the master key."

Angela produced her ID from her pocket, sliding it across the counter. She watched, only slightly more patient than Ruff, who was clad in his makeshift service vest. His whole body vibrated at her side as Mavis inspected the identification card with a scrutiny that would have given Chief Helbar a run for his money.

"Everything seems to be in order," Mavis finally said, handing it back. "If you'd follow me, please."

Angela's pulse mirrored the rhythmic ticking of the grandfather clock in the lobby as they moved closer and closer to the back area of the bank.

Mavis stopped in front of a large door, and she led them to another small, locker room-like area. Angela's gaze swept over the neat rows of safety deposit boxes that lined the walls as Mavis scanned the numbers for the right one. "Here we are," she said when they reached the tenth row on the right wall.

"Box 1027," Mavis's voice echoed in the confined space as she led Angela and Officer Townsend down the narrow aisle. She stopped before one box and gestured toward it, then stepped back to give Angela and Officer Townsend some privacy.

Angela's hands grew sweaty as she inserted her master key, twisted it, and turned it in the lock with a satisfying click.

As the door to the box creaked open, Angela let out a low whistle. Before her lay a stack of documents bound in twine, with several aged photographs peeking out from beneath the string. Angela and Officer Townsend exchanged significant glances. She reached out with trembling hands and began sifting through the photos.

They were a mix of candid shots and staged moments. To the untrained eye, they wouldn't think anything of them. A man shaking hands with another at a pier—was this the transaction point? A boat moored in the background—could it be the transport for forged artworks?

She flipped through them before sifting through the documents and pulling out her notebook to scribble notes: dates corresponding with suspicious bank transactions, names linked with coded messages found in cold cases from the precinct. This was way bigger than either of them had thought.

"No way," she breathed.

"This is impressive," Officer Townsend agreed, as he ran a hand down his chin. "How long do you think it took him to collect all this?" he murmured. His camera phone clicked rapidly as he snapped as many pictures as he could.

Angela shrugged. "Who knows?"

"He must've been involved in the ring for a long time."

Angela hummed as she reached inside and carefully split a pile of documents between herself and Officer Townsend.

A photograph slipped from the pile, fluttering to the floor. She stooped to retrieve it, and her eyes widened as she gasped.

"Everything alright, Ms. Atkinson?" Mavis called softly from her post near the door to the room.

"Perfectly fine, thank you," Angela answered.

"Take your time. Just let me know when you're done," Mavis replied with a polite nod.

Angela straightened up and tucked the photograph back into the stack, but not before showing it to Officer Townsend, who gave her a quizzical look. When she held it in his direction, his hand flew into his mouth. "No way. Is that...?"

Angela nodded. "Penny," she confirmed. "And I'll bet you anything the guy next to her is James."

Townsend nodded. "If that's true, it means Stirling has been plotting against these guys..."

"For years," Angela finished. "Exactly."

Townsend ran a hand through his hair. "Wow."

Angela kept digging, picking up one document after another, scanning for names, dates, and anything else that could help them unravel this web of mastermind criminals. Together, she and Officer Townsend sifted through every piece of evidence, gathering everything they could to take back to the station.

When they were done, Angela glanced at the contents one last time to confirm nothing was missed, and then the two of them carefully repacked the box.

Angela checked her watch as her pulse pounded in her ears. They'd been here more than an hour already. They needed to get this evidence to Chief Helbar as quickly as possible if they wanted to keep this trail from going any colder than it already was.

"Thank you, Mavis." she said, nodding at her as they made their way out of the vault.

"Chief Helbar will want to see this immediately," she said as she pushed open the door to the station, the familiar scent of aged wood and coffee lingering in the air.

***

"Angela, back so soon?" Kim looked up from her desk, then smiled when she saw the extra pep in Angela's step.

"Got something big, Kim," she said hurriedly. "Where's the chief?"

"His office, but he's on a call. Want me to—"

"No need, I'll catch him between thoughts," Angela replied, already moving toward the chief's door.

"Good luck," Kim called with a laugh. "Tell me everything later."

Angela didn't bother knocking. The door was already partially open, and as much as the chief didn't like to be interrupted, she figured he would make an exception for this.

"Chief, you need to see this," she announced.

Chief Helbar looked up, his eyebrows knitting together as he shot her a menacing glare before mumbling something into the phone and resting it with the screen side down as he swiveled toward her.

"Angela, I hope this is more than just another one of your hunches," he grumbled.

"More than a hunch, Chief." Angela slapped the documents from the safe deposit box onto his cluttered desk. "Evidence. Proof that Penny and James—or should I say Chandler—are neck-deep in this forgery ring."

The chief leaned forward, his gaze skimming over the material. His fingers reached out to brush over the glossy photos, as if they could tease out the truth by touch alone. "This is Sterling's safety deposit box haul?"

"Every last bit of it." Angela hovered at the edge of his desk, watching as the chief's demeanor shifted from skepticism to something akin to admiration. "Officer Townsend has more photos on his phone, but from everything here..." she took a deep breath and locked their gazes. "I think Walter's the one pulling the strings."

The chief cringed as he ran a hand down his face. "Well, if you're right. We're cooked." he arched an eyebrow and crossed his arms. "Walter has diplomatic immunity, remember?"

Angela nodded. "Yeah, but Chandler doesn't." She pointed to the list again, where his name was the second from the top. "And if I'm worried about his relationship with Penny, then we need to bring her in for another round of questioning. She might just be the perfect piece of bait to lead us to the big fish."

"Dang," Helbar muttered under his breath, pushing back his chair with a creak. "I'll have the boys bring her in. It's time to get them all."

Angela's lips pressed into a thin line as she tried not to smile. "I knew you'd see it my way, Chief."

"Doesn't mean I'm happy about it." Chief Helbar's gaze met hers. It was a mixture of gratitude and exasperation which only she could elicit. "You and Ruff stirring up trouble... makes me miss the days when the worst thing I had to deal with was teenagers tipping cows."

"Speaking of Ruff," Angela said with a smirk, "I'm thinking he might be ready to track. Officially. Could come in handy if we're dealing with runners."

"Your dog training antics are not official police business, Angela," he groused, but the twinkle in his eye betrayed him. "Still, keep me posted."

"Will do." Angela backed out of the office, leaving Chief Helbar to marshal his forces. So close. Now she just had to convince Penny to cooperate.

Chapter 23

T he sharp tang of fresh paint wafted up her nose as Angela approached Penny's studio. Her boots crunched on the gravel path as she adjusted the cuffs of her denim jacket.

Kim fell into step beside her and placed the hand on her shoulder. "We've got your back, Angela."

"Let's hope Penny's in a talking mood," Angela replied, her voice betraying none of the anticipation that raced through her veins.

They entered the building with gusto. The front appeared to be a bit of a ghost town, but Angela navigated the way toward the back office.

"Ms. Bedingfield? It's Angela Atkinson. We need to have a word."

It took a moment, but the door creaked open to reveal Penny, her auburn hair pulled back in a hasty knot, eyes wide with a carefully curated innocence that didn't quite reach her gaze.

"Angela, to what do I owe the pleasure? And the entourage?" Penny's words trembled a bit too quickly for her to recover as her gaze darted to Kim.

"The innocent act won't work anymore," Angela said curtly. "I know about Chandler. I know you're not telling us the entire story."

Penny's face paled. She glanced past Angela and when her gaze settled on Ruff and Kim, a flicker of panic crossed her features.

"Chandler? I don't—"

"Please, Penny." Angela crossed her arms, her blonde hair slapping against her cheeks as she sighed and shook her head. "No more games."

Penny's eyes darted toward the window and Ruff crouched down as if readying himself for another chase. But at the last second, she seemed to think the better of it. Her shoulders slumped, defeat creeping into every contour of her body.

"I don't know what you're talking about," she murmured again, but the tremor in her voice betrayed her. "I can't help you." She stepped back and was about to slam the door shut, but Angela moved closer and slipped her foot inside.

"Penny," she whispered, hoping a gentler approach might sway her mind. "I understand you're scared, but think about your son. He relies on you."

"Angela, please." Penny's eyes were wide as she shook her head. "You don't understand—"

"Talk to me, Penny," Angela urged. "We can't do anything if we don't know the complete story."

"Chandler—he was almost killed because he wanted to leave. If I talk, if they find out..."

"Your son needs you to be brave now, more than anything," Angela said.

"Brave?" Penny scoffed, even as her shoulders sagged. "What's brave about turning myself in?"

"Courage isn't always about facing down the bad guys in some dramatic showdown," Angela countered. "Sometimes it's about facing up to the mistakes we've made. It's about doing what's right, even when it's the hardest thing to do."

Angela held Penny's gaze even as she shuffled on the balls of her feet. "Consequences don't just disappear," she continued, "But facing them, accepting responsibility... that's how we make things right."

"Make things right?" Penny's laugh was brittle, hollow as it echoed through the studio. "I'm no hero, Angela. I'm just trying to survive."

"Survival's not enough when it comes at the cost of everything else. You're part of a community here. Your actions—they ripple out, affect people," Angela said.

Kim spoke up. "We can protect you. Both of you. All I need is your cooperation."

"Protection?" Penny's voice cracked as she clutched at her cardigan. "How can I trust you? You don't know what you're up against."

"We know more than you think," Angela said, gesturing between herself and Kim, who offered the young mother a kind smile. "And if you want the truth? You're standing at a crossroads. One path leads to more fear, running, looking over your shoulder every day."

Penny looked visibly deflated as her gaze met the ground.

"The other? It's a harder road, for sure. But it comes with a chance at redemption."

Kim nodded and stepped forward. "Penny, if you help us, I promise you that my chief and I will do everything we can to make sure you and your son are safe."

Angela watched as the internal battle played out across Penny's features—the instinct to flee, the desire to protect what was hers, and finally, a deep, long-buried yearning to unburden herself of the lies that weighed her down for so long.

"Okay," Penny finally exhaled. "I'll do it. For Ben."

"Good choice." Angela nodded, feeling the tension ease a fraction. There was still much to be done, but for now, they had a glimmer of hope—a starting point from which they could unravel the tangled web of forgery and deceit.

***

They pulled up to the station, but Angela knew from Penny's skittish demeanor she wasn't quite ready to face the music yet. Instead, Angela reached into the pocket of her worn leather jacket and produced a crumpled pack of gum. She offered a stick to Penny, who took it with trembling hands from her seat in the interrogation room.

"Chewing helps," Angela said with a wink. "Takes the edge off when the world's spinning."

Penny nodded, unwrapping the gum with fidgeting fingers and popping it in her mouth. The rhythmic motion of her jaw brought a measure of calmness to her eyes, and she offered the tiniest smile. "Thank you."

Angela smiled back.

"You'll do great, OK?" she assured her softly. "I've seen people come back from worst. There's a way through this, but you must walk it with us. You won't be alone."

"Will Ben be okay?" Penny's voice cracked as a single tear dripped down her cheek.

"He'll have your courage," Angela affirmed. "And he'll have a community that looks after its own."

Something akin to relief passed over Penny's features as she absorbed Angela's words. The tension in her shoulders eased, and she relaxed a bit.

"Alright," Penny breathed out, her decision made. "Let's go."

Together, they walked toward the police station, Penny's steps growing more certain with everyone's. Angela kept pace beside her.

"Kim will take it from here," Angela said as they entered the lobby, where Kim was waiting to lead Penny into the interrogation room.

"Ms. Bedingfield," Kim greeted Penny as warmly as she could, given the circumstances. "This way, please."

Penny hesitated for a fraction of a second before nodding, allowing Kim to lead her down the hall to the interrogation room. Angela watched them disappear around the corner and crossed her fingers behind her back. Hopefully, Penny would cooperate.

"You did good, Atkinson," Chief Helbar grumbled from his post near the front desk.

"Doing good is the simple part," Angela replied, watching as the door closed behind Penny and Kim. "It's living with the consequences that's hard."

When the door finally opened, releasing the pent-up tension into the corridor, Kim found Angela waiting at her desk.

"Penny came through," she said happily. "She gave us locations for Walter and Chandler. We might have a real shot at catching them now."

Angela nodded, her eyes mirroring the gravity of the breakthrough. "And Conrad? Michael?"

"No leads on them yet," Kim admitted. "But this... this is solid ground. We'll keep digging."

"Alright," Angela said as she exhaled and rested her head in her hand. "Let's hope Mother Nature's on our side and the tide turns in our favor."

"Nature—and a bit of good old-fashioned police work," Kim added, a wry smile twisting up the corners of her lips.

***

Angela's gaze swept over the aging corkboard in Chief Helbar's office. Her fingers traced the outlines of the freshly pinned map where red circles marked Penny's intel on Walter and Chandler, their ink still glistening under the fluorescent lights.

"Chief, we've got to move fast on this," Angela said. The chief, who had been shuffling papers on his cluttered desk, looked up, his eyes narrowing as he assessed the map.

"Agreed," he grunted, pushing away from his desk to stand beside her.

"Dell," Chief Helbar barked out without turning to look at the officer lingering in the doorway behind them, "you're taking Townsend with you. Hit these spots ASAP."

Kim gave a firm nod. "On it," she confirmed.

"Take care, Kim," Angela said, "and keep me looped in."

"Always do," Kim replied with a brisk smile, before swiftly exiting to gather her gear and rendezvous with Officer Townsend.

Chief Helbar watched her leave before turning his attention back to Angela. "You know, your old man would be proud of the way you handle yourself around these parts." His gruffness couldn't fully hide the speck of warmth that seeped through his words.

"Let's just hope we get to Walter and Chandler before they realize Penny's talked," Angela answered, brushing off the compliment.

The Chief nodded. "Keep me updated, Atkinson. And stay out of trouble."

"Trouble finds me, Chief. You know that," Angela shot back with a wry grin as she followed him out.

Chapter 24

The shrill ring of Angela's phone cut through the calm of her farmhouse kitchen. Still, no fresh updates from Kim on where they were with the Chandler and Walter lead. Last she heard, they were chasing them down a highway, but no one had been caught yet. She wiped her hands on a dish towel, leaving behind traces of flour from her morning scone-making endeavor (spoiler alert: epic fail), and picked up the receiver. "Angela Atkinson," she announced, tucking a loose strand of blonde hair behind her ear.

"Angela? It's Penny." Penny's voice was tinged with an urgency that instantly set Angela's nerves on edge.

"Hi Penny. What's up?" Angela steadied her tone, despite the flutter in her chest.

"It's Chandler," Penny gasped out. "He's been sending me messages, trying to reach me. He's scared, Angie. Keeps sending me his location, like breadcrumbs leading back to him."

"Locations?" Angela propped the phone between her shoulder and ear, reaching for a notepad and pen. "Have you saved them?"

"Every one of them."

"Good. Stay put, Penny. We might need you to help us bring him in."

A mere fifteen minutes later, Angela stood by the open gate of her farm, her gaze following the gravel path that led to the road. Troy Jeffries pulled up in an unmarked cruiser, its engine purring softly in the early morning.

"Morning, Angela," he greeted, her voice as bright as the glint of sun on the water. "Chief Helbar briefed me. Ready for a trip to Cherryville?"

"Let's do it." Angela locked the gate behind her, taking a moment to glance at the goats that milled about, blissfully unaware of the human drama clogging up her day. She climbed into the passenger seat, feeling the familiar thrill of a case pulsating through her veins.

"Townsend is meeting us there," Troy said, putting the car into gear. "Penny thinks Chandler might cooperate if we approach this delicately."

"Let's hope she's right," Angela murmured, watching the town blur past as they headed toward Cherryville.

The car's tires crunched over the gravel road, carrying Angela and Troy closer to the heart of Cherryville. The briny scent of the sea was faint but persistent. Angela rolled down the window, letting the cool breeze tousle her blonde hair as she considered their next move.

"Okay," Angela said, turning to face him, who kept his eyes on the road. "We need Penny to be our insider here. She can call Chandler and make him think she's ready to meet up."

Troy nodded, his grip tightening on the steering wheel. "But we must be careful not to spook him. If he smells a trap, he'll bolt."

"Exactly." Angela nodded. "We'll play this like chess. Just focus on his next move and go from there."

They reached the outskirts of Cherryville, where a row of houses sat shoulder to shoulder. Pulling into a nondescript parking lot, they found Officer Townsend with Kim waiting by his cruiser, the midday sun glinting off his badge.

"Officer Townsend," Angela nodded as she stepped out of the car. "We're going to use Penny to draw Chandler out."

"Sounds risky," Townsend remarked, scratching his chin.

"Risky, yes, but necessary," Angela replied, pulling out her phone. "Penny has agreed to help. We just need to keep her on track."

The trio huddled around Angela's phone as they dialed Penny's number, the ringtone echoing in the open air. When Penny's voice answered, it was laced with nervous energy.

"Angela?" Penny's voice quivered. "Is everything set?"

"Listen closely," Angela said, her tone firm yet reassured. "You're going to call Chandler. Tell him you want to meet. But whatever he says, keep him talking. We need to pinpoint his location."

"Can you do that?" Kim asked, peering over Angela's shoulder at the phone screen.

"I... I think so," Penny stammered. "I'll try my best."

"Good," Angela affirmed, her thumb hovering over the tracking app she'd booted up. "And Penny? Be convincing. We need this."

As Penny's fingers flew over her phone keyboard and the tapping echoed in the air, Angela's eyes didn't stray from the digital map before her. Gradually, dots appeared, leading them closer and closer to Chandler.

"Got something," Angela whispered after several tense minutes, tracing a line on the screen. "He's moving, but these locations are real-time. He's close."

"Let me see," Officer Townsend leaned in, squinting at the glowing dots. "That's the Sea Breeze Motel. It's run-down, mostly used by drifters now."

"Perfect place to hide in plain sight," Kim mused.

"Let's go," Angela said. "But remember, slow and steady. We need to bring Chandler in without causing a scene."

"Right behind you," Townsend said, as he and Kim climbed into their car.

With Penny still on the line, feeding them information, the team moved in.

Angela led the way across the Sea Breeze Motel's parking lot, her gaze locked on the second-floor balcony. The motel boasted peeling paint and salt-worn railings. Kim kept pace beside her, hand resting near her holster, while Officer Townsend and Jeffries brought up the rear, their eyes scanning for any signs of trouble.

"Room 12," Angela murmured, double-checking Penny's latest message.

"Let's circle around back," Kim suggested in a low voice, "less chance he'll spot us coming."

"Good idea," Angela agreed, adrenaline coursing through her veins. The foursome slipped between two buildings, where the smell of brine mingled with the musty scent of discarded seaweed from the nearby shore.

As they approached the back of the motel, Angela made out the distant barking of dogs from some far-off yard.

"Officer Townsend, confirm the chief is in position," Angela said without turning her head, her eyes fixed on the sagging staircase that led to the upper rooms.

"Backup's ready on our signal," Townsend replied after a brief pause.

"Okay, we go quiet until we're sure we have him," Kim instructed. "No need to spook him into doing something stupid."

"Roger that," Angela whispered back.

The four of them made their way up the stairs, the wood creaking ominously under their collective weight. Angela drew in a breath laden with the tang of salt air and mildew, reaching out to test the handle of room 12. Locked.

"Kim, your picks," Angela said softly, stepping aside to let the younger woman work.

"Got it," Kim replied, her fingers skillfully manipulating the lock picks. Within seconds, the click of the tumblers signaled their victory.

Officer Townsend gave a nod, and Angela's hand rested on the doorknob before she turned it.

"Police!" Kim shouted. "Open up!"

Nothing.

"Police," echoed Officer Townsend. "Open the door!"

Still no answer.

Angela twisted the knob, and the door swung open with a protesting groan, revealing Chandler and Walter in the midst of what looked like a heated discussion. Their expressions morphed into shock as Angela, Kim, Troy, and Officer Townsend made their unannounced entrance.

"Police! Don't move!" Townsend barked.

Chandler scrambled up from the edge of the bed, his eyes darting toward the window—an avenue of escape that was quickly closed off by Townsend's firm stance. Walter stood frozen behind a rickety table littered with papers and empty coffee cups.

"What is the meaning of this intrusion?" Walter sputtered.

"We're not involved in anything illegal," Chandler added quickly, his voice tinged with a note of desperation that didn't quite mask the underlying guilt.

Angela reached into her pocket and pulled out her phone. "Penny Bedingfield," she said, training her gaze on Chandler. "You remember her, don't you? She's been very... cooperative."

She tapped the screen a few times, bringing up a video chat with Penny. The image was shaky at first, then stabilized to show Penny's anxious face. Her eyes flitted about nervously, and she sucked in a breath when her gaze landed on Chandler before she regained her composure.

"Good evening, gentlemen," Penny said, with a surprising amount of grit in her words. "Seems I'm in a bit of a bind here, and I've had to make some tough choices."

Chandler's façade of ignorance crumbled as he watched Penny level their gazes. Walter, too, seemed to deflate slightly, the lines on his face deepening with the realization that their secrets were no longer safe.

"Chandler," Angela said, allowing her voice to soften just enough to offer a sliver of sympathy, "we can make things easier for you, but you need to work with us. You have a child to think about. Don't forget that."

A tense moment passed as Chandler regarded Penny on the phone, and Angela could almost see his gears turning. Walter, though red-faced and with his fists clenched at his sides, said nothing.

"Okay," Chandler murmured finally, his voice barely above a whisper. "What do you want to know?"

Angela nodded. "Where are Conrad Cummings and Michael Dunard?"

Chandler's shoulders slumped as he locked eyes with Angela. "Conrad," he said, "he's at the old mill on the outskirts of Cherryville. He's got this... set-up there." His voice cracked as Walter elbowed him in the ribs.

"Shut up," he hissed. But Chandler ignored him.

"Good," Angela nodded. Chief Helbar came out from his post in the adjacent room, cuffs in hand. "You're doing the right thing for your kid, Chandler."

The chief, despite his usual gruff exterior, handled Chandler with an unexpected gentleness. The metallic click of handcuffs closing around Chandler's wrists echoed in the sparse motel room. Angela caught a whiff of stale cigarette smoke lingering in the air, mixed with the salty tang of the seaside town's breeze that sneaked through the half-open window.

"Chandler aka James, you are under arrest for your involvement in the counterfeit art ring," Chief Helbar announced. "Anything you say can and will be used against you in a court of law. You have the right to an attorney. If you cannot afford one, one will be appointed for you."

Walter and Chandler exchanged a glance, a silent conversation passing between them.

"Let's get them out of here," Angela said.

"Ruff," she said quietly, and the dog's ears perked up at the sound of his name. "Watch them."

Always. Ruff had already positioned himself by the door, ready to bark at the slightest provocation.

Angela stepped out of the motel, Ruff padding close behind her. She watched Kim and Officer Townsend hustle to their cruiser, their departure kicking up a swirl of dust and loose gravel.

"Back to Hummings Hollow," Chief Helbar said, clapping his hand on Angela's shoulder.

"Ruff, in," Angela commanded softly, pointing to the backseat of her car. The dog obeyed with a soft bark and jumped into the back.

"Good work today, Angela," Chief Helbar said.

"Thanks. Couldn't have done it without your support," she replied.

As the lights of Hummings Hollow came into view, Angela allowed herself a small smile. Another case in the books.

"Almost home, Ruff," she whispered. "Almost home."

Chapter 25

T he mid-December chill nipped at Angela's cheeks as she strode up the cobblestone path to her parents' retirement home. A warm glow spilled from the windows, piercing the encroaching twilight. The familiar scent of roasting chicken wafted out as she opened the door, and a cacophony of familial voices greeted her.

"Angela! You're just in time; we were about to send out a search party," her father teased when she mounted the steps to the porch.

"Traffic was horrendous," Angela replied, shrugging off her coat. Her blonde hair cascaded freely over her shoulders when she removed her hat and mittens.

"Here, let me get that for you," offered Caroline, Angela's older sister. She whisked Angela's coat to the hall closet.

"Come sit by me, Angie," beckoned Abigail, patting the cushion next to her on the floral sofa.

"Mom, how are you feeling?" Angela asked, taking the offered seat with a grin.

"Never better," Abigail said, waving off the concern with a flick of her wrist. "You know what has perked me up? That new Christmas tree farm they've opened down by Miller's Creek."

"Really?" Angela leaned in, intrigued.

"Absolutely. Remember how we used to take you all every year as kids? Pick the tallest tree, sip on hot cocoa, feet freezing?" Abigail's face relaxed into a reminiscent smile.

"I used to love that place," William chimed, joining them from the kitchen, a wooden salad bowl cradled in his hands.

"You sure did," Abigail laughed. "It's important, you know, keeping these traditions alive. Especially now, when everything else seems so... fleeting."

Angela watched as the flicker of the firelight touched upon Abigail's features, casting shadows that seemed to amplify the lines of worry that hadn't been there last Christmas. Her mother's eyes held a wistfulness that tugged at Angela's heartstrings.

"We need to make every moment count," Abigail murmured, almost to herself, before she caught Angela's gaze.

Charlie reached over, squeezing Abigail's hand gently, his own eyes darker than they had been before her mother's diagnosis.

Caroline's lips pressed into a thin line and William stood by with the salad bowl still in hand. His posture straightened, but his expression softened as his gaze drifted to their mother.

"Hey, now," he said, breaking through the somber mood. "Let's not forget the new star attraction at this year's Christmas fair—the giant snow globe you can actually go inside! I hear it's quite the spectacle."

Abigail's lips curved into a small, appreciative smile as she turned toward William. "Is that so?" she asked. "I hadn't heard about that."

"Absolutely," William replied, placing the bowl on the table with a flourish. "They say it's like stepping into a winter wonderland. Snowflakes the size of cotton balls!"

Charlie chuckled. "You planning on trying it out, Will?"

"Maybe I will," William retorted with mock bravado, "if I can brave the lines of squealing kids and their exhausted parents."

Laughter bubbled up around them, and Angela felt a sense of gratitude for William's knack for steering them away from more serious topics. The air grew lighter, tinged with the aroma of roasted chicken and herbs.

"Speaking of spectacles," Caroline piped up, her tone conspiratorial, "did any of you see Ruff herding the geese in town yesterday? He's getting really good, thanks to Eggatha and her chicks."

"Ruff's becoming quite the farm manager," Angela added, grinning at the thought of her dog taking his duties so seriously that even the geese fell in line—albeit with a great deal of honking and flapping.

"Only because he's got an excellent trainer," Charlie said, giving Angela a knowing look.

"Or maybe it's just his natural charm," Angela teased back.

As they chatted, Abigail's fingers danced over the crinkled pages of the Hummings Hollow Gazette. She had picked it up off the coffee table, scanning for a splash of festive green and red. "I want to find that new Christmas tree farm ad," she muttered. "We should go back this year."

"Should be in the lifestyle section, I reckon," William suggested.

"Ah, here we—oh!" Abigail paused mid-flip. A bold headline stopped her cold—Geoffrey Thorne Art Gallery: Grand Re-Opening under New Ownership. The accompanying image showcased the familiar facade, now repainted in vibrant colors. "Look at this. Old Thorne's place has changed hands?"

"Really?" Caroline leaned over and peered at the paper. "Good. That gallery needed a breath of fresh air."

"Hope they keep the charm," Charlie added with a nod.

"Angela," William said, turning toward her, "did you ever get to the bottom of that epergne business? And what about Conrad?"

She nodded and readjusted her position on the couch. "Yes, we found it," she replied, her voice carrying a note of triumph that she hadn't expected to feel so strongly. "Conrad's part in it all... well, let's just say justice has a way of catching up."

"Good on you, Angela," William said, his eyes crinkling with pride before he lifted the bowl of vegetables, passing it along. "Couldn't have happened to a more slippery fellow."

"Indeed," Angela agreed, as everyone gathered around the table and the conversation shifted from art galleries to ill-gotten antiques.

Angela reached for a buttery roll, her fingers brushing against the cloth napkin as she spoke. "Kim and Officer Townsend caught Conrad just in time. They nabbed him before he could cross state lines with the epergne." She passed the basket of rolls to her father.

"Conrad," Caroline muttered, shaking her head while reaching for the pepper shaker. "I always knew there was something fishy about that man."

"Once he realized his cronies were already behind bars, Conrad's tune changed pretty quick," Angela added, as her butter melted into the roll. "Started singing like a canary, hoping to get on the chief's good side." She paused and then winked. "It didn't work, of course."

"Justice and self-preservation," William said, raising an eyebrow. "Strange bedfellows, but I suppose fear makes people do strange things."

"Exactly," Angela confirmed, meeting his gaze. "Fear has a way of showing someone's true colors."

Angela sliced through her chicken. As she chewed thoughtfully, the rich aroma of rosemary and thyme from the garden wafted through the dining room. "Then again, he had little choice in the matter," Angela added. "Sterling was poisoned, but Conrad says he did it with his back against the wall."

William leaned forward, his brow furrowed. "What do you mean?"

"Threats came from Walter and Chandler—the big fish in this forgery pond," Angela explained as her fingers absently traced the grain of the wooden table. "They held debts over Conrad's head. He feared for his life, so he acted out of desperation." She shook her head and let out a long breath. "But that doesn't excuse what he did. There's always a choice, however dire the situation may seem."

"Still," Charlie chimed in, his voice carrying a hint of sympathy, "it must be a weight off to know those two are caught and can't harm anyone else."

"Absolutely," said Angela, a soft sigh escaping her lips as she thought of the closure it brought to Valentina Balducci. "And Valentina has the epergne back now, so everything is right where it should be. Well, except for Walter, but the chief says he'll work with the courts to fast-track his deportation."

"Goodness, I remember when her family first lost it," Abigail said, her face brightening at the mention of the artifact. "The collection meant the world to her. It's comforting to know there's some justice after all."

"Justice and a bit of peace." Angela smiled faintly.

Angela reached for the bowl of mashed potatoes, her hand brushing against Charlie's as he passed it to her.

Ruff poked his nose over the top of the table and stole Angela's last piece of chicken.

Charlie let out a hearty laugh, slapping his knee. "That dog of yours is something else. Takes after his owner, I'd say—tenacious and a bit too clever for his own good."

Angela smiled. "Maybe," she mused. "But I wouldn't have it any other way."

END OF BOOK 9

OTHER SERIES: Jasmine Moore is a local favorite who is unusually gifted—she has random visions of the future that often portend disaster. She can also understand her loyal golden retriever. Literally. When a body is discovered in the small town of Blackwood Cove, Jasmine's instincts tell her that there's more to the story than meets the eye. Taking up the mantle of detective, she sets out on a path full of twists and turns to solve the baffling case.Sifting through decades of forgotten town history and long-buried secrets, she soon discovers that everyone has something to hide...Time is running out, and Jasmine needs to unearth the startling truth before the town is shaken to its core yet again.

"The story has a Nancy Drew style to it... fun and upbeat with a mystery that's intriguing, engaging, and is perfectly fitted to the witty duo of Luffy and Jasmine... funny, charming, lighthearted"--**5 Stars, Readers' Favorite**

Paws in the Action **is the first book in the Pet Psychic Cozy Mysteries series. If you adore intriguing cozy mysteries with quiet seaside towns and a sprinkling of the paranormal, then you won't want to miss out on Jaz and Luffy's fun and unforgettable adventures.**

Paws in the Action is now on Amazon

FREE NOVELLA: A roaring blizzard. A rest area in the middle of nowhere. Seven strangers stranded with a dead body. The killer is close by, and no one's going anywhere. In Cold Case, there are secrets lurking in the snow.

Join Max Parrott's author newsletter and get *Cold Case* for FREE

Dear Reader,

Thanks for helping Angela and Ruff solve the case! If you have enjoyed the book...

...could you kindly leave a review?

Thanks, Max

P.S. Reviews are like giving a warm hug to your favorite author. We love hugs.

Leave a review HERE

Made in the USA
Coppell, TX
19 September 2024

37480892R00085